The Divas That We Are!!

The Divas That We Are!!

If you know your worth, others will recognize it and respect it.

By Temeka Monique

Copyright © 2012 by Temeka Monique.

ISBN: Softcover   978-1-4691-7737-3
            Ebook   978-1-4691-7738-0

All rights reserved. No part of this book may be reproduced or transmitted in any form or by any means, electronic or mechanical, including photocopying, recording, or by any information storage and retrieval system, without permission in writing from the copyright owner.

This is a work of fiction. Names, characters, places and incidents either are the product of the author's imagination or are used fictitiously, and any resemblance to any actual persons, living or dead, events, or locales is entirely coincidental.

This book was printed in the United States of America.

To order additional copies of this book, contact:
Xlibris Corporation
1-888-795-4274
www.Xlibris.com
Orders@Xlibris.com
112825

CONTENTS

Fairy Tale 15

Third Wheel 23

Breath of Fresh Air 33

Sex, Sex, Sex 43

The Situation 52

Keep Your Hands to Yourself 64

Lost 78

Her 82

Who Am I 95

The Things We Accept Be the Things We Regret 104

Let Me Reintroduce Myself 118

This book is dedicated to the man that put me on my way.

Special Thanks

To my family and friends, who supported me over the years.
Thank you, I couldn't have done it without you!

Author's Note

I set out to write this book with entertainment as its purpose only, but as I was writing I decided to put a message in the story. Many of you will get a different meaning of this book. Everyone's situation is different so some may take something out of this story that others won't. What I want most is that it empowers you to do whatever you need to do and know that you are special and always deserve the best. If you know your worth others will recognize it and respect it.

The characters in this story are fictional and do not describe actual people or events.

Introduction

The phone rang. It was Monique, calling to see what Isis was doing for the New Year. They had been friends since they were preteens.

"Hello?" Isis answered the phone.

"What's up, girl?" shouted Monique.

"Nothing, what are you doing?" asked Isis.

"Size nine, please," Monique said to someone else. "If you have nine and a half, you can bring that too, thank you."

"Where are you at, shopping again?" asked Isis.

"Yes, I need some new shoes for tonight," replied Monique.

"Where are you going?"

"I don't know, but I want to look good anyway. Happy New Year!"

"It isn't New Year's yet," observed Isis.

"So happy New Year anyway. Where are you going tonight?"

Just as Isis was about to answer the phone beeped. "Hold on," Isis replied, "it's the other line. Oh, it's Leah. Hang on, I'll tell her we'll call her back."

Leah had been friends with Isis and Monique since high school.

"Hey girl, what's up?" asked Leah.

"Mo is on the other line. Hang up and I'll call you right back so we all can talk." instructed Isis.

Isis clicked back over. "Mo?"

"Yeah."

"Hold on, I'm going to call her now."

The phone barely rang once before they heard a loud, "Happy New Year! What's up, ya'll? What are you guys getting into tonight?"

Isis quickly answered, "Monique is shoe shopping—*again*—and I'm at home cleaning. I want to bring in the New Year with a clean house."

Leah questioned Monique, "Mo, *where* are you at?"

"I'm in the mall trying on shoes to go with my outfit for tonight," Mo answered.

"Where are you going?"

"I don't know, but I want to be look *fabulous*." They all laughed.

"Isis, what are you getting into tonight?" inquired Leah.

"Nothing. I'm staying home with the kids. I never go out on New Year's. People are crazy out there. I'm just waiting for 2004 to end and 2005 to begin. This is going to be my year."

"I hope that 2005 will be much nicer than 2004," said Monique.

"What's your New Year's resolution, Leah?" asked Isis.

"I want to lose some weight and just be a better person," Leah answered.

"What about you, Mo?"

"I'm perfect. What do I need with a resolution?" she answered.

Laughing, Isis asked her once again: "for real, what is it? You know you're a mess!"

"To stop smoking cigarettes," answered Monique.

Monique asked Isis, "What's yours?"

"To love myself."

"Deep, girl. That's a good one," answered Leah. "So are you going to stay home?"

"Yes."

"If you change your mind, call me. You can go out with me—one of the girls from work is having a party."

"That would be nice," Monique interjected. "Go out, you're always in the house. Live a little!"

"No, I'm really OK," replied Isis.

The fact of the matter is that even if she'd had plans, she wouldn't have gone out. She was waiting to see if she got a phone call from Dashad. He was her world, but he had a family—a woman and two children kind of family.

As Monique and Leah continued their conversation, Isis thought to herself, how *did I get here*?

"Well, ladies," Isis finally interrupted, "I must get dinner on the table. I love you both, and I'll call you when the ball drops." They returned the gesture and ended the phone call.

She wasn't fooling anyone; everyone knew that she was waiting on him.

Isis turned the stereo on and chose a track that suited her mood: Mary J. Blige singing "No Happy Holidays."

"Five! Four! Three! Two! Happy New Year!" everyone shouted as Isis and her children watched the ball in Times Square fall. They made their ritual toast with iced tea with a hint of lemon.

No more looking back, Isis thought to herself. *2005, here I come*! But deep down, Isis knew she had to look back—to make sure she wouldn't lose her way again.

Chapter One

Fairy Tale

My name is Isis. I am a thirty-three-year-old divorced woman and the mother of three beautiful children: two daughters and a son, ages fourteen, twelve, and four. I know: what was I thinking? I was married young. I met Amin when I was seventeen and he was twenty-one. It was love at first sight.

I first saw him when I was getting off the bus one sunny summer day. He was on the corner of my block were all the guys hung out, including my brother. I remember it like it was yesterday. He stood out from everyone in the crowd. He was nicely dressed, very crisp. He had on multicolored, button-down polo shirt, deep black jeans, and clean white Reeboks. His hair was cut low and wavy, well kept. He stood about six foot two, with nice broad shoulders. He was a nice-looking brother. You could definitely tell he wasn't from around here. The other guys were dressed in their thug gear—you know, the baggy jeans hanging off their asses and T-shirts with slogans on them. They were rowdy. He stood quiet, observing his surroundings.

As I walked down the sidewalk, I could hear several different conversations going on. As I got closer, it got quiet. Everyone knew who I was because of my brother. I smiled, waved, and kept it moving. For a moment, our eyes locked. I knew once I walked past that everyone would be looking, and I was hoping he was, too. You couldn't miss my ass. I was five foot six and one hundred and fifteen pounds—in all the right places—with peanut butter brown skin, big beautiful eyes, a button nose, chipmunk cheeks, a bright smile, and long limbs.

I only lived a block from the corner. When I walked into my mother's house, my brother Rochine was watching music videos and eating his favorite hoagie, turkey and cheese.

"What's up?" he said.

I didn't give it a minute to find out about the mystery man on the corner. I knew that my brother would know who he was. He knew everything that went on in the streets. Even if he wasn't there, he would know exactly what went down.

"Do you know who that guy is on the corner?" I questioned.

"Who?" he asked.

"The one with the polo shirt. He ain't from around here."

My brother thought for a minute about who I could be talking about. I stood there patiently, waiting for an answer. He finally responded, "He's not. Why are *you* asking?"

"Shut up! I just wanted to know. Who is he?" I demanded.

"Some cat from Philly. He's Chris's cousin," Rochine told me. "Stay away from them."

"I knew it," I yelled. Then I said, "You ain't my dad," and stormed out of the room.

My brother was three years older than me exactly; I was born on his third birthday. For some reason, he thought he owned me. My mom and dad split when we were young, so he looked out for me. My mom was a nurse and works crazy hours. I had another brother, Jaylin, but he was much younger than us—he was seven years old that summer. So it was pretty much me and my brother Rochine.

I called my favorite cousin to see if she had seen this beautiful man or had any more information about him, since my brother wasn't letting me in on anything.

"Hello?" Aurora answered.

"What's up? I called you earlier; where were you?" I demanded.

"James came by to get me and the baby. We went to the park and then got some pizza," she explained.

Aurora was my first cousin, my mom's sister's firstborn. We were tighter than tight. She was nineteen. We had been best friends all our lives.

She had a one-year-old baby, Amaris, by this guy name James. Amaris was so pretty, like a china doll. That was about the only thing that he had done right.

"That's nice of him, to start acting like a dad," I said sarcastically.

"Don't start. He's trying."

"Yeah, Amaris is one now. He's behind, way behind. But I'm not going to talk bad about your daughter's father. I called to see if you wanted to go to the mall with me."

"What did you get?" she asked.

"Some sunglasses, that's it. You know I hate to shop alone. But I didn't want to stay in the house. Plus I wanted a smoothie."

"Was anyone up there?" she asked.

"No, but let me tell you about this guy I saw on the corner."

"*Where?*"

"By the stoop. He's from Philly."

"How you know?" she questioned.

"Roe told me. And he told me to stay away from him, which made me want to know more. He is so cute. What are you doing? Come over."

"Nothing, but the baby is taking a nap."

"When she gets up, come over." We hung up.

After we got off the phone, I went to sit on my front porch to read the latest gossip in the weekly tabloid magazine until my cousin came over. I hadn't been on the porch even five minutes, and guess who was walking down the block on the opposite side of the street? Yes, Mr. Philadelphia. I was trying not to look, but how could I ignore him? He even had a nice walk.

I couldn't believe it; he was parked right in front of my house. He must not have seen me at first. He was into his own thoughts, I guess. He was about to get into his car, which was a green 7 Series BMW with chrome rims. When he noticed me on the porch, he tilted his head back as if to say *what's up?* I smiled and gave a wave. I believe that gave him the OK to come closer and talk to me.

"How are you doing?" he asked.

"I'm fine," I replied. I was so nervous. I was hoping he couldn't tell that I was. I didn't know what to say to this guy.

"You live here?" he inquired.

"Why?" I snapped back.

"Because I'm parked in front of your house," he replied calmly.

"Oh yes, I live here." I changed my tone quick.

"What's your name?" he asked.

"Isis. Isis Williams. What's your name?"

"Amin, just Amin." He laughed.

"What's so funny?" I questioned.

"I can tell I'm in Jersey."

"Why you say that?"

"You gave me your first and last name. Where I'm from, you're lucky to get someone's real name."

"Where are you from—and is Amin your real name?"

"I'm from Philly. And yes, Ms. Isis, Amin is my real name. What do you like to do?" he asked.

"What are you the FBI or something?" I was wondering what was with all of these questions. I didn't have an answer for that one. I hoped that I didn't come off to strong. He must not know my age, because if he did, he would know that I hadn't done much to have a favorite thing to do.

He smiled. He had nice teeth. "No, I am not the FBI."

I had to change the subject. "What were you doing on that corner with those bums?" I asked him. "They're trouble."

"I came to check on my cousin," he answered.

I didn't know what else to say. I could barely believe that I, "motor mouth" as my mom called me, didn't have a word to say. This had never happened to me; usually I was the one talking. He interrupted my thoughts. "You never answered me."

"What was that? I asked.

"What do you like to do?" he asked again.

"I like bowling and going to the movies." He didn't have to know that I only did those things with my cousin or my family. "I also like to read."

"We have a lot in common, I like to bowl and go to the movies, and I love to read. How old are you?" he continued with the questions.

I knew I couldn't escape that question. "I'm seventeen."

"When is your birthday?"

"October twentieth. I'm a Libra."

"So you'll be 18 soon."

"Yes. In about three months."

"Yes," he repeated. "I like how you say yes."

"How old are you, and when is your birthday?" I questioned.

"I'm twenty-one, and my birthday is November fifteenth."

"So you have a birthday coming soon too."

It was quiet for a moment. I guess it was a lot to take in.

"What are you reading now?" he asked.

"I trusted them."

"I read that one. It's a good book . . . hey; can I get in touch with you later? As a matter of fact, take my number. You can call me." He went into his car and got a pen, then wrote down his number on the back on an insurance card and gave it to me. He told me that he was sorry he didn't have more time to speak with me: he had somewhere to be. As he got into the car, he rolled down his window and said, "Call me later—you're not as mean as they say you are." I smiled, and then he pulled off.

Just then my nosy brother came out on the porch. "What did I tell you?" he scolded. My reply was, "Shut up. He was just being friendly."

Before he could reply, Aurora turned the corner, saving me from my brother's mouth about my new mystery friend. Perfect timing.

Later that night I called Amin. We talked all night long. Neither one of us wanted to get off the phone; he was just so nice. But that's all we did was talk on the phone. He said he didn't want any trouble with my mother or brother. Plus, he would be ready for me by the time I was eighteen. I didn't understand what that meant, and I didn't ask any questions.

I would see his car parked in front of my house at least twice a week, and would come out to see a dozen red roses on the porch each time. He became my best friend, and I was his. We shared all our goals and dreams. Weeks went past and our relationship grew, still only over the phone. The weather was changing. Summer was over; it was fall. I loved the fall season—the leaves changing, the pretty colors, just the mood that it brought.

One week before my birthday, Amin asked me what I wanted. I told him to surprise me. He did just that. The morning of my birthday, my mom came to wake me up, all excited. Someone was at the door for me. It was Amin. I was shocked because had never come to the house for me before. My mom knew of him from the roses and from our talks, but had never met him. He had introduced himself to her and told her of his intentions before she came to wake me. I hurried to the bathroom to freshen up, wondering what was going on. I came down into the living room, and he smiled.

"Good morning, baby."

"Hey, Amin," I said uncertainly. I was nervous; my mom looked on, smiling.

"What are you doing here?"

"Happy Birthday!" he shouted.

"Thank you."

Then he pulled out a black box and got down on one knee and asked if I loved him.

"Yes, I love you," I said in my sleepy voice.

"What are you doing for the rest of your life? Whatever it is, I want to do it with you. Will you marry me?"

I just stood there, looking at him in amazement. A few seconds went by.

"Baby?" he said, trying to get my attention. He had it, but I was just stuck. He opened the box to reveal a two-carat princess-cut diamond ring. It was beautiful.

I couldn't believe it.

"Will you marry me?" he asked again.

"Yes! Yes I will," I replied, smiling from ear to ear. He got up and kissed me for the first time. It was like cotton candy melting in my mouth. It was so sweet. I had been waiting for that kiss since I had laid eyes on him. Then he turned to my mother and gave her some airline tickets. He told her that we were going to Jamaica to get married, and he would love it if our families could be there. My mother needed a vacation anyway; she worked very hard to provide for us. I couldn't believe this was happening to me. I called Aurora to tell her what was going on. He informed me that we would have to go meet with his family. While I was getting dressed, my mom and brother sat down and talked with Amin. I was so happy.

He took me to meet everyone. His mother and his sister welcomed me into the family. He had a big family—aunts, uncles, and cousins. It was a lot of people to meet. They were all so nice to me.

One week later, both of our families set off for Jamaica. It was beyond a story book wedding. It took place in the early afternoon, in a gazebo on the beach. The rich sand was warm under our feet. Water crashed on the rocks below. You could see the water for miles, clear blue with no end in sight. Our families looked on as we exchanged our vows. It was priceless. I wore a cream and peach sundress. My hair was swept up in curls with an exotic flower on one side. Amin wore a cream linen short set. Everything was so beautiful. I went from being Isis Nyree Williams to Mrs. Amin Nasir Richardson.

I spent a week on this beautiful island with my new husband. *Someone wake me*, I thought to myself. *I have to be dreaming*! I had never been pampered in this fashion before. I was waited on hand and foot by the best staff, and I ate the most scrumptious food. It was truly the best honeymoon.

After we got back home, he had another surprise for me. He had bought a home for our family in the suburbs of Jersey. It was a four-bedroom colonial, with a two-car garage and a big, fenced-in backyard just like I had dreamed of one day having. It was lovely. I couldn't believe it.

"I just want the best for you," he said.

"Thank you, but you gave me the best when you married me."

No wife of his was going to work, so we started on our family. Eleven months later, Amirah was born. Two years after that came Amir. I had my girl, and he had his boy. He was a great father. We were so happy, until the day I got a phone call from Amin: he was in jail. My husband was sentenced to ten years in prison. I was left to fend for myself and my children. I had never had a job; I was truly a housewife—Suzy homemaker. I took care of the family and household things. The most I knew about finances was writing checks and sending them out before the bill was late. Our savings only lasted about two years, with the lawyers and paying the taxes on the house. It was rough for awhile, but I did find work—two jobs, actually.

As the years went on, my husband and I grew further apart. In the fourth year of his sentencing, he asked for a divorce. He said it wasn't fair for me to go on like this, for my life to be put on hold because of something he did. He closed himself off to me and the kids. He wanted me to move on; he said the time would go by faster for him. Some people would agree with that, but I didn't and don't. I was devastated; the only man that I had ever loved didn't want me anymore. I was sick; I threw up for days. I didn't eat. I completely fell apart. My mom came to stay for awhile to help me out, but no one and nothing could take away the hurt I was feeling. I was devastated, I tell you. But you know that we as women don't know the strength we hold until we really need it. I had to get myself together: I had two children that I had to take care of.

For about two years I focused on me and my children. I decided to follow my dreams and become a chef. I provided a wonderful home for my children and started to live again. I met someone we'll just call

Romeo—he really thought he was a Casanova. We dated for two years and spoke of marriage, but he was never really ready. We had a child: a little girl, Anya. Six months after she was born, we separated. It seemed that he couldn't keep his dick in his pants.

Well, I thought, *back to the drawing board*. This time I was going to make it work for me. I had another mouth to feed, but God had carried me this far, and I was sure he would continue to bless me. He did. Six months later I opened a little restaurant called Meeks, A nice family restaurant with good, home-cooked food.

The restaurant took off, but I had forgotten about love and companionship. I was busy making a life for me and my family. I thought I would never love again; never find what I had with Amin. That kind of love is priceless! Then I met Dashad, the remix of Amin. I really liked him; he reminded me of what I had lost. *Who knows?* I thought, *maybe the third time is the charm*! Dashad stood six foot one and weighed just over two hundred pounds. He was solid as a bull, with a caramel brown complexion—he was Jamaican and Cuban. He had curly black hair and beautiful brown eyes with long eyelashes: very handsome. He was educated, owned his own business—a legal one—and spoke three languages; he had been all over the world. He was perfect, ladies—*perfect*! I absorbed him like dry sponge to water. The devil comes in many disguises.

Chapter Two

Third Wheel

It was the last week in June, and Leah asked me to be the third wheel.

"I met someone!" she said, excited.

"From *where*?" I said with a disapproving tone.

"Delaware. We're going down there tonight."

"You are. I'm not."

"I don't want to go by myself—please?"

"I can't go. I have this wedding on Saturday. I can't be playing around with you and your new knight in shining armor."

"You'll be back tomorrow afternoon. I have to work, too. Please? He's so nice. You need a break anyway."

I was silent. She was right—I did need a break. "All right, since you're begging."

"Thank you, thank you! I'll be over at seven. See ya!" I looked over at the clock; it was 4:30 PM. I didn't have much time to get ready: so many things and so little time. I had to call my mother, cook—no, order out—and still be beautiful for whatever was about to come my way.

Leah arrived looking nice, wearing khaki capris, a low-cut shirt, and sexy wedge heels. She stood five foot three and had nice shape, but more bust than butt. Leah is a redbone: she looks like Faith Evans to me, could be her sister. She had that around the way girl style. The positive black woman attitude.

She was rushing me from the moment she got to the house. I told her to give me a minute and go see her godchildren. After ten minutes, she yelled up the stairs, "Come on, we have to get gas before we get on the highway."

"Why didn't you do that before you came?" I asked.

"I didn't know if you were going to drive," she explained.

"I am not taking my truck: this is your little adventure. I'll drive up, and you drive back."

"OK, but come on."

She wouldn't come upstairs because she knew we would be up there for another half an hour. I gathered my things and came downstairs.

"You look good—damn, girl, can your ass get any bigger?" she hollered out.

I had on a gray and white velour Roca wear short set that I had brought from one of the stores on South Street. The shorts took to the shape of my ass. I had on some low, strappy white sandals, my hair was pulled back in a long, sophisticated ponytail, my nails were French-manicured, and my makeup was flawless.

"Shut up! Thank you, and let's go," I said.

I gave the kids kisses and hugs, gave my mom last-minute instructions that she wasn't going to follow, and we were out the door.

"Do you have good directions?" I asked. "I don't like getting lost."

"Yes."

The drive didn't seem that long; we talked the whole way, catching up on our lives. Lately, we hadn't had time to kick it. We both had children and careers. Leah had two children, a boy and a girl. Both were my godchildren.

She told me how she had met the man we were going to see; Bryan was his name. Leah was a manager at a clothing store. One of her employees was having a birthday party and invited her to this club in Philly. She said it was nice: I would have liked it, an upscale adult crowd. She described him as having a dark complexion—chocolate. He was very cute, about six foot tall, with a stocky build and big feet. We laughed. She said he seemed like he had his stuff together. He was an owner of a sports apparel store. He had two children from a previous relationship, but never had been married. She was hoping Bryan would be the one to change her luck with men. She was tired of meeting momma's boys, wannabe gangsters, and drug addicts in denial.

We finally pulled into the parking lot at the Marriot. She called him on the phone and let him know that we had arrived. Within fifteen minutes, he had pulled up in a black 5 Series BMW with tinted windows and rolled down his window. He *was* cute. She introduced us, we said our hellos, and he told us to follow him. It was about nine o'clock. The town that we were in seemed quiet. It had a lot of stores with local names. It looked like a quaint little town. Soon we arrived at an apartment complex occupied by working people. You could tell by the cars that were parked in the numbered spaces: Hondas, Toyotas, and Chevrolets—nothing as fancy as the car he was driving. As we pulled into the space next to him, Leah looked at me and said, "Isis, please behave."

"What the hell—I'm five now?" I replied.

"No, but you know how you can get," she explained.

"Shut up. We're going to have a great time."

As we got out the car, he hugged Leah and told her how happy he was to see her again. He showed us the way in, down a long hallway to his apartment at the end. He opened the door, and we proceeded in.

"Have a seat," Bryan told us. "Would you like something to drink?"

"No thank you," Leah said.

"And you, sorry—what's your name again?"

"Isis. No, thank you. Could I use your bathroom?"

"Yeah—second door to the right."

I had to use the bathroom bad. We'd been in the car for over an hour, and I wanted to check my makeup. No, I didn't look in the medicine cabinet. You've seen that commercial. I could hear them talking; he was asking how was the trip, and did she find the directions to be easy. When I came back out, they were still talking. I sat down and started to look around. It was a nice, two-bedroom apartment, clean, with many pictures on the wall: Malcolm X, Muhammad Ali, some scenic pictures of the seasons and the ocean. As I looked around, I noticed a water machine. *Plus one for Bryan*, I thought. He must have been into his health, which is always a good thing.

The Wire was on the television, so I watched that while they talked and tried to include me in their conversation. Bryan's phone rang. "What's up? No. Yes. No, all right," he said. It was hard to tell who he was talking to, whether it was a man or a woman. We looked at each other, thinking the same thing. I was hoping that it was someone on their way so I wouldn't have to sit here all night looking at this television. I could have watched *The Wire* at home with my mom.

"Can you take a ride with me?" he asked.

"Yeah," Leah responded.

"It won't be long," he explained. Before long, we pulled up to the back of a plaza, and he got out and ran inside. I guess it was his store. He had to close up the store. After about fifteen minutes, he came out with another guy. Bryan was holding a night deposit bag. The guy and Bryan talked for a minute.

I told Leah, "I'm hungry. You rushed me down here, and I didn't have time to eat anything." By now it was 10:30 PM.

"What's open now?" she asked.

"I don't know. A convenience store? Even this town should have one," I said.

"Ok, I will tell him." Leah said.

Then Bryan got in the car and the guy got in his truck. We drove off at the same time. We went to the night drop box and proceeded back to the apartment. As we were driving back, we passed a Wawa, but Leah never opened her mouth. We returned to the bachelor pad.

Bryan walked in first, then Leah second, and then I followed. I shut the door and proceeded in. I was startled by a gentleman sitting on the couch in the living room with the television off. He was deep in thought. He spoke to Bryan and Leah, and gazed at me before saying hello. Bryan introduced us to his friend; his name was D. Yes, just the letter D. I hate that. Just say your name, and then when you get comfortable with someone, you can tell them what you would like to be called. He offered his seat to me.

"Thank you," I said. Bryan and D conversed for a minute, and then excused themselves to the other room. That was perfect, because I wanted to let Leah have it for not stopping at the store. Now my stomach was growling.

Leah looked at me and said, "Cute." She was trying to butter me up.

"Why didn't you tell him to stop?" I questioned. Just then they came in the room to inform us that they would be right back. Of course I spoke up: "We'll be back also. I'm sorry, but I didn't eat anything before the trip here."

D said that he would take care of it; we should just order something, and he would pick it up and bring it back. That was so sweet. He suggested Chinese, being that it was so late. I agreed. Once they left, Leah looked at me and said, "Please don't start."

"Don't start what? I'm hungry. What, we can't be hungry? I told you I was starving earlier. You trying to be cute, is that gonna make a bad impression if I'm hungry?" I scolded.

"What you mean trying? I *am* cute!" We laughed. We had been friends so long we argued like we were sisters. She changed it up fast: "What you think about D?"

"Can't think about anything right now—I'm too hungry. Let's order."

"What do you want?" she asked.

"Shrimp and broccoli," I replied. She wanted Chicken and broccoli. She called Bryan and told him we had placed the order, and they had said ten minutes. He let her know he was on his way to the Chinese store now. They came back shortly after. I was so happy now my stomach wouldn't be touching my back anymore. They had also visited the liquor store.

"Thank you."

"You're welcome," he said.

"Would you like some?" I asked.

"No thank you," he replied. We sat at the table and began to eat. They sat on the couch. After he saw that I was finished eating, he asked me, "Where are you from, Isis?"

"I'm from Jersey. Are you from out here?"

"I live here, but I'm from New York. I grew up in Florida, though. I want to make it back there someday."

Leah had moved to the other side of the room with Bryan. They were off into their own conversation.

"So what is it that you do?" he asked.

"I'm a chef; I have my own catering business," I replied.

Leah interrupted: "The girl can cook her butt off."

"A chef?" D questioned. "What are your specialties?"

"Everything," I smiled. "Seriously, I love to cook. I put my signature on everything I cook. When you love your job, you will always be the best at it. What is it that you do, D?" I asked him.

His reply was "I own a barbershop."

"Are you a barber?"

"No, I just own the shop."

"How long have you been a chef?"

"About five years now."

The conversation went on all night long. We talked about business, politics, and our children. After he found out we had so much in common, he put his hand out and reintroduced himself to me.

"My name is Dashad," he said. I smiled.

"Nice to meet you," I replied.

Much to my surprise, I was intrigued by this man. Besides all that we had in common, we were the same signs, the same birthday month, only ten days apart. We liked the same foods, and our favorite restaurants were the same. Most of all we loved the same ice cream—Heavenly Hash—and I think we were the only ones on the planet who ate it.

As the evening—well the morning—grew later and later, I was hoping he wouldn't ruin it by trying to get some ass. I was hoping that he was different. I seen potential in him, but I said a little prayer anyway, *please let him be a gentleman all night*. Then I excused myself to the bathroom. When I returned, he was on the couch. I sat next to him, and he extended his arm out and touched the small of my back when I sat down. It felt wonderful. His hands were soft and strong. I knew he had been waiting all night to feel my silky smooth skin. I didn't act fidgety, but I was uncomfortable. What would he try next? As I turned to position myself to get comfortable, I made him spill his drink. I got up to get paper towels, and as I looked back at him, he was looking dead at my ass. I asked him "Are you all right?"

He brought his head up to reply, "It's OK. It didn't spill that much."

"Here you go." I gave him a wet paper towel and a dry one.

"Thank you."

I was getting tired now: it was three in the morning. I couldn't believe that we had talked that long. It had been a while since I had enjoyed the conversation of the opposite sex.

"I think I'm going to call it a night before I make another mess," I explained. I meant getting involved with him on the first night, hours after I met him. Who makes these rules anyway? Before I started to the guest room, I thanked him for his company and for babysitting. He said it was his pleasure, and that was that. We didn't exchange numbers: I guess he was there to keep me clear of Bryan and Leah. As I lay in the bed I thought, *could I see myself with this man, could it work*? It didn't matter, though. I was too chicken to give him my card.

The next morning, bright and early, I was up. I came out of the room, and to my surprise Bryan was asleep on the couch. He has earned some more cool points. He didn't even push, that was smart. I proceed to the bathroom to get ready. I was in the shower when Leah came in, "Good morning."

"Good morning," I replied.

"How was your evening?" she asked.

"Very nice, thank you. You were right, I needed a breather," I answered.

"*So how was your evening?*" I asked.

"Nice, clean, respectable. You see where he is, right? We chuckled.

"Dashad was nice . . ."

She interrupted "Oh, Dashad?"

"Shut up, we have a lot in common," I continued.

"So?" she asked.

"So what?" I asked her back.

"When are you seeing him again?" she continued to drill me while she was brushing her teeth.

"What do you mean?"

"You didn't give him your number?"

"No."

"Why?"

"For what?"

"You just said so yourself: you had a lot in common."

"He never asked for it."

"What did you say to him?"

"Nothing. Leave me alone about this. I came up here for you, not to find a boyfriend!" She washed her face and left the bathroom. I think she was upset with me. I know she meant well, but it was my life. I finished my shower, left the bathroom, and went to the room so I could get dressed.

While I was getting dressed, I called my mother to check on things. Everyone got off to school on time and she was at the store already. My mother is my lifesaver.

"Did the deliveries come in?" I questioned her.

"Yes they did, just got here."

"Did you check them . . ." She cut me off. "We got this. We know what we're doing. Roe is here with me. Just relax, and I'll see you when you get here."

"Thank you, Mom, I love you. It's not that I didn't trust you; it is that everything has to be in order. This wedding is very important. We'll be on the road shortly; I'll call you when I'm home."

"OK." We hung up the phone.

I finished getting beautiful and packed my bag. I made the bed and came out into the living room. Guess who was waiting in the living room with a smile? Dashad—and he definitely got some cool points for this—wasn't going to let this opportunity pass him by.

"*Good morning!*" he said. I smiled and replied, "It is a good morning."

"I brought you some tea." He reached for a cup off of the counter and handed it to me.

"Thank you, that was sweet," I said.

"How did you sleep last night?" he asked.

"I slept good, and you?" I inquired.

"No, I didn't sleep well, I was thinking of you all night," he told me.

That was it: I couldn't stop smiling. I was speechless.

"I really enjoyed you last night. I haven't had that in a while. A real conversation," he explained.

The truth is I was thinking about him also, but I figured he didn't ask me for my number so I figured he didn't want to be involved.

"I enjoyed myself last night also. It is very hard to have an interesting conversation with someone nowadays," I said.

He *was* smart and cute, and he had earned many cool points last night; maybe I could give him my number. Maybe I could give him a try.

"I added milk and sugar," he said.

"Thank you, just the way I like it. How do you like your tea?"

"The same way, and with fresh-baked bread. I have had it every morning since I was a kid," he explained.

Leah and Bryan came into the kitchen. Dashad said good morning, then began talking to Bryan about some meeting he had later on that day. Leah and I walked off to sit in the living room.

She whispered, "Did you check on things?"

"You know I did," I said smiling. "Everything is fine. The children were to school on time and the deliveries were there on time, too."

"Is someone opening the store for you?" I questioned.

"Yeah, Natasha. I asked her just as a backup," she explained. "So we're not in a rush?"

"No," I said.

"Looks like you came down here and got yourself a boyfriend," she said, smiling and looking into the kitchen where Dashad was standing.

I smiled. "Yeah, let's see if he makes the cut. So far so good." I began to sip my tea. It was delicious.

We gathered our things and started to say our good-byes. Dashad brought my things out to the trunk.

"Here's my card. I would like to see you again sometime soon—if that's possible?" he questioned, standing there looking so good.

"I would like to see you also." I gave him a card out of my bag. "Here is my card. The best way to reach me is by my cell phone."

"OK, I'll do that." He hugged me and gave me a kiss on the cheek, and told me to drive safe. I let him know that Leah was driving; I got to relax. I hurried Leah up as said her good-byes.

Before we got back onto the highway, we had to stop to get some Dunkin Donuts coffee. I needed some coffee and a croissant. The tea was nice, but I needed my morning drink. I loved Dunkin Donuts coffee; Leah was a fan of Wawa coffee. She said it was better. I did not agree. Starbuck's is too strong, makes me want to climb a wall. D & D has the right blend. We drank our coffee and exchanged our views of the trip on the way home.

"Seem like he's feeling you?" Leah asked with a grin.

"Funny thing, he really thought he was going to out-talk me." We both laughed.

"Do you think you'll see Bryan again?" I asked.

"Yes, girl, again, again, and again," she replied with a devilish grin.

I thought to myself that Dashad was nice, and when he touched me, I did feel something. "I could see him again," I blurted out. Leah asked, "Are you ready?"

I said nothing. The conversation changed to our lives. She was contemplating firing one of her employees. The girl was slow; Leah would give her a project, and it would take her forever to complete. She was always late and had to leave early. Leah scolded her, and the girl snapped back at her. She spoke with her and wrote her up. I suggested giving her another chance; she may been having a bad day. I was an optimist. I tried to see the good in all people. We were all human. We all made mistakes. Anyway, I had been Leah's friend since forever, and I knew how she could get on someone's nerves. She always had to be the HBIC—and we all know what that stands for. There are always two sides to a story.

My mind flashed back to Dashad. Could this be the start of something special? Could he be what I had been praying for in a man? We were almost to my house. It had felt good to get away, even for that little bit of time. *Now back to work*, I told myself, *my mini vacation is over*. We pulled up in front of my house, I got out, and Leah popped the trunk.

"Well, love, thank you for the *breather.*"

"You are so very welcome. But really, thank you for coming with me. I will call you tomorrow," she said.

"OK, drive safe," I said.

I opened up the door, "Honey, I'm home." I laughed; I knew no one was home. I loved coming into my house; it smelled like apple jack and peel. I loved the tranquility of being home. I put my bags on the floor, took my shoes off, and just flopped on the couch and enjoyed the peace for a moment. Just then, my cell rang, "Hello?" I said.

"Yes, may I speak to Isis?"

"Yes?"

"It's Dashad."

"Oh, hi."

"I was calling to see if you made it home safe," he said.

"Yes, I just got into the door. I am sitting here gathering my thoughts before I head out to the store. Busy day today; I have a wedding this weekend. I'm looking forward to Sunday, so I can get some rest," I replied.

"Well, I just wanted to check on you. When you have a minute, give me a call," he said.

"I'll do that. Talk to you later," I told him. I then called my mother at Meek's.

"Hey Mom. I'm home and on my way shortly," I said.

"Hi, baby. Can you stop and get some flowers for the tables?" she asked.

"Yes, see you soon." I hung up.

So refreshing to be completely relaxed when you go to work. My day turned out to be very organized. I was too busy to think about Dashad. By the time I got home with the kids and played catch-up, I was ready for a bath and bed.

Chapter Three

Breath of Fresh Air

My cell phone rang. I picked it up to see who was calling me so early in the morning. It just said "Incoming call." I answered it anyway.

"Hello?" I said.

"Hello, how are you this morning?" said the familiar voice.

"I am good, and you?" I questioned the stranger on the other end of the phone.

"You don't know who this is, do you?" the voice questioned.

"No, I can't say that I do. But your voice sounds very familiar," I answered.

"It's Dashad."

"Oh, how are you this morning?"

"If I could see your beautiful face for lunch, it would be a great morning," he said with his deep, sexy voice. How could I turn him down? Just the sound of his voice would make anyone melt.

I kept my composure. "Lunch?" I questioned.

"Yes, lunch. You do eat? Please don't tell me you keep that figure of yours by starving yourself?" he asked.

"No, I eat. Of course I eat. I am a chef. What time were you thinking? I have a couple of things to do this afternoon," I explained.

"Well, Ms. Lady, you are in luck. I have cleared my whole schedule today just to see you. What things do you have to do?" he asked.

"My daughter has swimming lessons at 1:00 PM till 2:30 PM at the Y. I usually work out while she is getting her lessons,"

"Do you mind if I join you?"

"Do you work out?"

"Yes, I also have a membership at the Y, and I would love to meet your daughter." Dashad said.

I paused. I was thinking if it was good for him to meet Anya so soon. Was he moving too fast? Just then, he interrupted my thoughts.

"Hello?" he broke the silence.

"Yes, I am here," I answered.

"Does that sound like a good idea?" he continued to ask.

"I am thinking," I said.

"I like that."

"Like what?"

"That you are thinking. Thought shows signs that you are smart. You don't just jump into things," he said.

"That sounds like a plan," I said.

"Where should I meet you?" he asked.

"You can meet me there around 1:30. I like to watch her for the first thirty minutes, and then I work out for the remainder of the time there. It is right off the highway, so it will be easy for you to get there. Once you leave, call me so I can give you directions."

"I'll call you once I'm on the highway."

"Okay, talk to you then. Bye."

After I hung up the phone, I thought of how it had been a year since I had been on a date. I did want to see him. What would I say? What would we talk about? Did I really want him to meet my baby? She would detect if he was no good on the spot. He called me, so he must be interested. I don't have to make him like me. It was going to be in a public place, so I wouldn't feel uncomfortable. I relaxed a little, jumped off of my bed, and headed into the bathroom to get ready. As I looked in the mirror at my reflection, I wondered if I was ready for this. Was he who I had been praying for? There were so many questions. "Relax, you got this," I told myself.

Just then I heard the pitter-patter of little feet.

"Good morning, Mommy," said Anya.

"Good morning. Are you ready for swimming today?" I asked her.

Her eyes lit up. "Yes!" she said with excitement.

"Go get your suit on so we can eat breakfast. You hungry?" I asked.

"Yes."

"Go get ready. Brush your teeth and put your suit on and meet me downstairs."

She went flying out of the room and down the hall. She loved the water. She was like a fish.

We ate breakfast. We had pancakes and eggs and sang songs. I tried to spend time with each of the children individually, so one day out of the week Anya and I had "Mommy and me day." We went to her swimming class and then had a lunch of her choice. It's good to give children choices. It stimulates their thought process.

After breakfast, we were out the door. I had to stop at the restaurant first. We weren't open for customers, but my bees were busy.

"Good morning," I said to my staff.

"Good morning," they all replied. My employees loved me: I was good to them. I walked over to the head chef, my brother Rochine, and asked him where my mother was.

"She's on the phone, I think with the Matthews party," he replied.

As I walked in my office, my mother was indeed on the phone. She mouthed "Matthews" to me as she pointed to the phone. I just smiled. I set Anya up at her little station in the corner of my office to color and play while I took care of some paperwork and invoices.

"Yes, Mrs. Matthews, that won't be a problem. I will see you tomorrow night. You have a blessed one. Thank you. Bye."

My mother was such a help. She just knew what to do and how I would like it done without asking me. You always need someone on your team that knows you and knows what to do without asking. She knows me the best.

"Good morning, Mother. I see you are on the ball," I said as I kissed her cheek. "What would I do without you?"

"Go crazy," she said laughing. "Mrs. Matthews just added fifteen more people to the party. Okay. I am stopping by her house tomorrow with samples and to pick up the deposit."

"Has she decided on a date?"

"No, not yet, but she definitely wants to book you. We will also discuss that tomorrow. It looks like sometime in August."

"Book *us*, Mother! I am nothing without my team," I scolded. "Okay, please bring me up to speed."

"First, tell me how your trip was."

"Mom, it was nice. Yes, I met a man."

"I know."

"How? Leah called here for me?"

"No," Just then she started toward the walk-in freezer. She opened the door and came out with a big bouquet of roses. "These came for you this morning. You must've made some impression on him."

All I could do was smile. They were beautiful. There were sixteen full-bloom cream roses with peach tips on the tops. Just beautiful. They must have put the roses in water that had peach dye in it, and then when they turned color, they transferred them back into plain water. I had never seen roses like them. I took the card out and opened it. It read: "I wanted to brighten your day, being that you have brightened mine. See you later. D."

My mom was just standing there, waiting for details.

"He's nice. He is meeting me today. We are going to work out together," I told her.

"He is driving over an hour *just* to work out with you? What magic did you put on him?" she said with a smirk.

"You know the baby's lessons are today," I explained. "He asked to have lunch, but I told him I was going to work out, so he wanted to join me."

"I am only kidding. I am happy that you have found someone interesting enough to exchange conversation with. You deserve to be happy; you work hard enough," my mother said.

"Now, Mom, about work?" I asked.

While she was talking, I couldn't keep my eyes off the beautiful display of roses. She went on about the invoices that needed to be sent out, and how I needed to look over the inventory and do the scheduling for the events that are coming up. I looked at the time. We had to go.

I was a little nervous. What would we talk about? I hadn't watched television in two days. I didn't even know what was going on in the world. I had been so busy. Just then, my phone rang. "Hello?"

"I'm here. Are you inside?"

"No, we are pulling up now. So you got here on your own? Very impressive," I said.

When I pulled up, I saw him standing outside of his car. It was a gray Maxima SE with black leather interior. I gathered Anya and my things and got out of the truck. He walked over to us and introduced himself to Anya.

"Well, hello there," he said to her. She smiled and waved and then looked at me.

He grabbed our things. "Hello."

"Hey," I said. "Glad you made it."

"Me too," he said. We walked into the building, and then we separated. He went into the men's locker, and we went into the women's locker. After about ten minutes, we came out to the poolside. Dashad was already sitting on the bleachers. *Wow*, I thought, *he is just on it, just how I like it*. He waved to make sure I saw him. I walked over to Anya's instructor, said hello, and then went to sit down on the other side of the pool to observe the children. I sat right next to him. We watched Anya for about twenty minutes and then proceeded to the gym to work out.

"I usually get on the treadmill to warm my body up first, and then I switch to different stations," I said. It seemed like he was following me. It didn't matter what we did first, second, or third. I got on the treadmill, and he got on the one beside me and ran while I walked.

"Your daughter is so pretty," he said.

"Thank you," I said. "How was the drive?"

"Very relaxing," he said.

"Thank you for those beautiful roses. They are very pretty. I have never seen roses like that before," I said.

"You're welcome. I haven't seen them. I just called a local florist in your town and ordered them. I told them they were for a beautiful woman who I had just had the pleasure of meeting. She assured me they would send their best. I must call and thank them."

"That was really sweet," I said, smiling.

The fact of the matter was that I hadn't stopped smiling since I had laid eyes on him. He was a pleasant breath of fresh air. So different, so cute. A man. What would I do with him? I didn't have time for myself. I felt him starting at me.

"You look good when you sweat; it makes your skin glow. It's sexy," he said, complimenting me.

I just smiled: what can you say to that? I was mad that I was sweating.

I changed the subject. "So how old are your girls?" I asked.

"Eleven, nine, and three," he said.

"Do you see them much?" I asked.

"The two older ones live in New York with their mother. I see them every weekend—almost every weekend—and I see my youngest daughter every day. I take her to school and pick her up," he replied.

"So what do you do besides cook?" he asked.

"I like to bowl, the movies . . . the usual stuff." I replied.

"What's the usual stuff?" he questioned.

"I don't do much outside of my family and the restaurant," I explained.

"Well that is all about to change," he said.

Did he know something that I didn't? I guess so. I couldn't help but stare at him: he was so rich. I don't mean money. His skin was so smooth, his hair was deep and dark like midnight, his eyes could make you just relax at a glance.

"What do you like to do?" I questioned him.

"Relax," he said simply.

"Well what do you do to relax?" I pressed.

"I play pool, I go to the batting cages sometimes, and I play basketball," he informed me.

We switched stations as we casually chatted about things that were going on in the world. I was glad that he was talking. He was filling me in on what I had missed in the last couple of days: politics and chaos.

"How many times a week do you work out?" he asked.

"Just Thursday, when Nya has her lessons. I don't have the time. Plus it doesn't make sense to leave and come back, and I want to be here if anything ever happened," I explained.

"God forbid," he said. "It's just that you look like you work out all the time."

"I think I stay slender by being in motion sixteen hours a day. How many times do you work out a week?" I said.

I knew he worked out; no man could have that body and not have worked at it.

"I try to go three times a week with Bryan and some of my other friends, who you will meet shortly," he said.

I just smiled and got off the machine. *Good*, I thought, *he has plans for me in the future*. It was about time to go back and get Nya. I told him I would meet him in the front lobby.

While we were getting changed, Nya decided on Chuck E. Cheese for lunch. She loved it there. I got a lot of work done while she was running around, so it benefited both of us.

We walked out and there he was, just standing there looking good. There were a few other women in front of us, and I caught them studying my beautiful man-to-be.

"You ready?" he asked.

"Yes, we have chosen Chuck E. Cheese for lunch," I told him. Nya was jumping around in excitement. He began to smile. "Let's go, I'll follow you."

We got into the truck, and he got into his car. We arrived ten minutes later at Chuck E. Cheese. We went in, and after I got her the tokens, Nya was off. I saw some of the other mothers from Nya's swim class there. They were looking like they were surprised to see me with a man. It was so obvious, even Dashad noticed it. "Do we have a bomb strapped to us?" he said.

"You notice that right."

"What would you like?" he asked.

"Sorry?"

"Do you want salad or pizza? Not too many choices here," he said laughing.

"Oh, salad. I'll come with you," I replied.

He ordered plain pizza, and he also ordered the salad bar for us both. He handed the lady the money. "Thank you, but you didn't have to do that," I said.

"No, it's my treat, just treating my ladies to lunch," he said.

He snuck that one in there: he knew what he was doing, and I liked it. After we created our dishes, we sat down.

"So how long have you known Bryan?" I asked.

"About eight years. He's a cool dude. You ask that because of your friend?" he asked.

"Yes. I have known Leah all my life, since we were kids. I love her and wouldn't want anything or anyone to hurt her," I said.

"I understand that. Bryan is a good guy," he explained.

The conversation went on, and Dashad told me he would like to get to know me better. Nya kept running to the table for more tokens or a bite of her pizza. I let him know that would be nice because I wanted to get to know him more also.

"How about dinner?" he asked.

"Tonight?" I asked him.

"Yes, I can't seem to get enough of you. I don't want to part with you," he said. He was saying all the right things. Was I dreaming? I let him know I had a couple of things to do later, but would love to have dinner with him that night.

That seemed to work for him. His father's mother lived in the city, and he wanted to visit. When I was ready for our date, I would just call him. He had it all planned. I loved a man who knew what he wanted, and it was clear that Dashad wanted me. Quiet as kept, I wanted him, too—in all ways. We went our separate ways, and I got back to what I was supposed to be doing. I went home and got things ready, then went to the restaurant. Everything was OK; my mother was on the job.

I called a sitter; I didn't want to alert the media that I was going on a date. She said she would be there at 6:30 PM. That was perfect: I was meeting D at 7:00 PM. We were meeting at Benihanas. I love hibachi. I couldn't help myself: I felt seventeen all over again. Was I falling for this man?
"Mom, the phone!" shouted Amirah. "I got it," I shouted back. "Hello?"
"Who has been a busy bee?" it was Leah.
"I was just thinking the same thing. I *am* tired," I said.
"You should be, girl tell all," she demanded.
"Tell you what? There's nothing to tell. He's nice," I told her. I really wanted to tell her that I wanted to jump up and down like I'd hit the lottery. But I had to remain cool.
"I just spoke to Bryan; he said D is down there with you," she replied.
"He sent me some cream roses. They're so pretty. The ends of the petals are peach. I've never seen anything like that before. That really made my morning," I explained.
As Leah talked, I kind of faded out—not intentionally, but I was on cloud nine. She was telling me about how her associates were airheads and she needed to fire them all. I was watching Nya on the slide. Children's lives are so simple.
"Hello?" she butted into my thoughts.
"Yeah, I'm here. I'm going out with him tonight, too. He has family in Philly that he's visiting. We're going to meet up later," I said.
"That is so good. Bryan assured me that you were in good hands," she said.
"That's funny, Dashad told me the same thing," I told her.
I explained to her that I needed a nap and promised to call her with all the details tomorrow. I needed to recharge, get my mind right. So much was going on. I laid down for about an hour. My cell woke me up: it was D. "Hello, beautiful," he said.
"Hello, yourself," I said.
"Just want to confirm with you—7:00 PM at Benihanas?" he asked.
"Yes," I responded.
"OK, see you then."

"Until then." Then I hung up.

I got off the phone feeling great. I went to check on the children. Everything was fine. I started to get dressed. I decided on casual fly. It didn't take long, either. The sitter arrived, and I was out the door.

When I got to the restaurant, he was already there. As soon as I came in the door, I could see him at the bar, smiling with delight. He was clean-shaven and wearing a nice shirt and dark blue jeans with causal shoes; he was put together. I liked that; he had his own style. He had ordered me my drink before I got in the door, I guess, because moments after I sat down they brought it over.

"Apple martini, right?" he said.

"Thank you, you pay attention. You are just on time with everything," I said. I sipped on my drink.

"How is it?" he asked.

"Perfect," I replied

"You been here long?" I questioned.

"No, about ten minutes."

"What are you drinking?" I asked

"VSOP, Hennessy," he said.

We sipped on our drinks, and he told me of his visit with his grandmother and family. He hadn't seen them in years. He told me he would take me to meet them one day. Soon our table was ready. It seated eight, but we had it to ourselves. I saw him slip something to the host as he sat us.

"Enjoy," said the host, smiling. As he walked away, I saw the fifty dollar bill in his hand. That turned me on. We sat down and looked at the menu. I chose the fillet and lobster tail, and he chose the same. We *did* have a lot in common. I guess it was because we were born under the same Libra moon. We continued to sip our drinks as the chef came over to introduce himself and check to make sure our order was right. As he prepared the food and did his little tricks, I could feel Dashad admiring me. I was smiling so much that my cheeks began to hurt. We watched the chef prepare our meal, placing each item on our plate for us to taste. Dashad ordered us another drink, and started to eat. We talked about our businesses and plans to make more money as we ate our meals. He was smart; I could learn a lot from him. This was the man I had prayed for.

"I really like you," he said. I smiled because of the way he said it.

"*I like you too,*" I said with a giggle.

Just then the waitress came over, and she asked me if I would like dessert. I declined. I was stuffed. He told her to bring the check.

"Tonight was wonderful. I really enjoyed this," I said.

"Anything you want or need, I'm here for you. I've never met a woman like you, and I don't plan on letting you out of my reach," he explained.

I smiled, thinking that he wanted me. I wanted him, too.

He paid the check and we walked out. He walked me to my truck.

"Thank you again," I said.

"It was my pleasure," he said.

We kissed on the lips—only for a moment, but enough to be wanting more. *Slow down, girl*, I thought. He opened the door for me, and I got in. We said our good-byes and left the parking lot.

I got home, and everyone was asleep—even the sitter. I took care of her and then went upstairs and got ready for bed. I watched the recap of the local news. I called Dashad to see if he was OK driving home. He was just about home, so I could go to sleep. He told me he would call me tomorrow. I turned the television off and started to fall asleep, thinking about how much work I had to do tomorrow.

It was Friday, the day before the wedding. You could only imagine how busy I was. I didn't even think about taking a break, there was so much to do in so little time. My main focus was on the wedding: no time for love today. I had to prepare for 250 guests.

Chapter Four

Sex, Sex, Sex

It was Saturday, the day of the wedding, I was nervous, but as always everything turned out perfect. My staff made me proud. I thought about when Amin and I had gotten married. I wished the couple a lifetime of happiness, hoping that that wouldn't change in the blink of an eye.

Once I got home, I was beat, but I wanted to call D and let him know how much of a success everything was and how much I had missed him. I got into the shower and fell out on my bed.

I woke up Sunday morning refreshed, and saw that I had missed a call from Dashad. My mom had plans with the kids for the day, so I decided to go see him. I drove down to his house this time. When I got there, I could not believe it: he was preparing pancakes for me for brunch. He said I had been working so hard catering to other people that someone should cater to me. I was so loving this man. He had a spread of fruit—every fruit you can name, he had. It was so nice. We had breakfast together, feeding each other without forks, just using our hands. It was so exotic. I can taste the mangos still. It was turning me on. He leaned across the table and asked me if I was his. I said, "Of course," and that was all she wrote. He began to tongue me down. His kisses made me want to take off my clothes. We were all over each other.

He scooped me up and carried me into his bedroom. He laid me on the bed gently. We continued to kiss and caress each other. Then he stopped suddenly. "I have something for you," he said. "Now?" I questioned. I wanted him to give me something else. He left the room and after a little bit he came back with a CD in his hands. He put it in the stereo and looked over at me. Piano keys started to play, and then I heard a woman's voice. It was Ashanti's "Baby." As I listened to the first chorus, the sultry music just took over—baby, baby, baby, baby, baby.

He came to me and put his lips on mine, and we got lost into each other. The song just kept repeating. He handled me like he knew what I loved. He undressed me like he was a pro. He took his time exploring me, applying just enough pressure to my body. First he massaged the front part of my body, and then he turned me over. He wanted to get familiar with every curve of my body, and he did just that. As he kissed me from head to toe, I ran my fingers through his curly locks. I couldn't believe it, it was about to go down. He kissed me on my neck and behind my ears. He quickly learned that that was my spot; it sent tingles through my whole body. As he positioned himself on me the kisses got deeper. I loved the eye contact. It was like I was the most beautiful woman in the world; he never took his eyes off of me. When he entered me with his full thrusts, I took him in like he lived inside me and had been away on vacation. He was home. He fit like a glove. He explored my sugar walls like he was on a treasure hunt. I don't know what he was looking for, but he found many treasures and treats. I caressed his body, rubbing my hands over every inch and lightly digging my nails into his skin. I didn't want to miss anything. I licked his body like he was a Häagen Dazs chocolate ice cream cone. It was total ecstasy. He had me all over the place; it was as if we were going in a clock motion all around the bed. We stayed at three o'clock for a while, and then he moved on—tossing and turning me, bending and pulling. We moved together like we had been husband and wife for years. I loved how he handled me. With each stroke, I was falling in love. This was it: he was amazing. He was a sex God. I came over and over, and he was loving it, too. We were both moaning and enjoying each other. He had discipline: no minute man here. He was all over me, and I was all over him. I hadn't had sex in so long I thought I would forget how, but it comes right back, like riding a bicycle. He had me in so many positions I didn't even know my legs could go that far into the air. As we were coming to the end, I could feel him getting bigger inside of me. When he came, he held me so tight. That was the best sex that I had had in a many years. Bravo!

We lay still and held each other as we got our bearings together; that was a lot to take in at once. He told me how great we were, smoking hot. I had to agree. He got up to go to the bathroom and get a washcloth so we could clean up. I couldn't move. I just lay there in amazement. He woke up every sense I had. I felt on top of the world. As he was walking out of the room, he stopped in the doorway to ask if I wanted some water. Just then, the smoke alarm started to go off. It startled the both of us, and then he just looked at me and smiled. "Told you we were hot!" he said with a smile, then proceeded out of the room. I couldn't believe it: his body temperature had set off the damn smoke detector. Really, most smoke detectors don't detect smoke; they detect heat. The chemistry was out of this world. We cleaned up and lay naked in the bed until we went to sleep.

Hours later I awoke to Ashanti's voice: "I got a jones forming in my bones, for a man who indeed took over my soul." I couldn't have said it better. I looked over at Dashad. He was still sleep. He was so beautiful. I snuggled up to him, his warm naked body against mine.

I awoke to him looking at me, smiling. I just started for a second, and then smiled back. He kissed me and got off the bed. I followed his perfect ass out of the room with my eyes. He came back in with some water and a bowl full of ice. I smiled as he gave me the glass and asked him what was the ice for?

"For you," he said."

"For me?" I questioned.

Then he came over and kissed me, and we were back at it again. I loved it: after all of that, he still had more in him. He rolled me over on my stomach, and then started dripping the melted water from the ice on my back. It was shocking. He had many tricks. He then put the ice in me—yes, there. It was erotic. When I came it would splash like I was a water faucet being turned on.

He was so romantic, not into rushing, just pleasing. He wanted to please me. It was great because it relaxed me and made me want to give more of myself. I did just that. He had the first round, but I damn sure got the last round.

We lay there exalted. I was upset that I would have to leave soon; I had a long drive, but I was so happy that I came. We got into the shower, and we didn't talk. We just smiled. We had done the damn thing, and done it well. He wanted to go out to eat some dinner, but I had to get back. I knew it would be another two to three hours before I got home. I called my mom and let her know I was on my way. He told me he would make it up to me, missing dinner.

I arrived home excited to see all of my babies and to hear about their day with my mom. They were just as excited to see me as I was them. We ordered pizza and watched a movie, and gabbed until we all fell asleep on the couch.

The next day was routine. I dropped everyone off and did my early morning errands. I paying bills, prescription refills, returning e-mails and voice messages. Monday was a busy day for me, but I was so relaxed. I really needed to just let go, but it is so hard sometimes. I wanted to call D, but I didn't want to scare him off. I'll *just call him later on tonight*, I thought.

I called him later that night. He was out with Bryan and his friends having drinks, but he told me he would call me once he left. I wondered if they were talking about me. Yes, I was full of myself. He did better than call; he showed up. I was really shocked, but very pleased. We had never chilled at my house. It was around 10:00 PM, so the kids were asleep. We had a late dinner; I whipped up some Salmon and rice with vegetables, and we shared our thoughts with each other about the day and our first sexual encounter. I felt comfortable with us in my house. I had thought I would be nervous but I wasn't.

I showed him around the house, showing him photos of my family. He commented that we had great genes. He always found a way to compliment me, and I loved that about him too. Not only was he feeling my beauty outside, he was digging the inside structure. I walked over and gave him a big kiss on his juicy lips. He just smiled.

We went upstairs to my room. He liked the layout of the room and my big bed, which we didn't waste any time getting into. He was just so amazing; he had so many tricks and treats. We explored each other again, but this time with a little more intensity, more feeling.

I was falling for him fast, and I didn't care. Every time it was something different, something new. He kept me very interested in him. We went out every day for 30 days straight. He was falling for me, too.

Each day we would go out of town, him taking me to one place after another. His dates were extraordinary. He said he wanted to give me every flower there was, if he could. On one of our dates, he did. He took me to the botanical garden in New York. There were so many flowers, plants, trees, and small animals. I saw a black squirrel; I had never seen one of those before. It was so pretty, all the colors mixing together, the best display of flowers I had ever seen. That is what I loved about Dashad—yes, loved. I was there, in love. He wanted to give me everything, the best. This would be something I would hold onto forever.

As we walked the path holding hands, we got deeper into the beautifully planted jungle. We walked, and he talked about his childhood. I just listened, wanting to absorb all of him, his memories and all. I was happy that he wanted to share his life with me. We came to a path that led down to a small, shallow stream below. He led as I followed him down. We sat there, talking and laughing on a big rock. He told me he felt like he was Tarzan, king of the jungle, and I was Jane. How sexy. We got into it right there in between that rock and a tree, in the open wilderness, free from the world. I thought it couldn't get any better.

I loved the feeling of the forbidden. We weren't supposed to be making love out there; we were supposed to be observing nature's beauty. We added to it with the beauty of a man and a woman making love. It was priceless. After we got done, we hurried and put our clothes back on before someone walking the path would see our naked bodies down by the stream. It was amazing. I could not express the emotions going through my body. It felt so good. Now I was at the point where I would just stare at him in amazement. He had me right where he wanted me.

After we left the garden, we went and got dinner before we headed back home. We went to a restaurant called Sam's, one of his favorite restaurants in New York. It was nice, very cozy. Once we were seated, I excused myself to the bathroom to freshen up. When I came back, he had already ordered our drinks. He had a Heineken—I guess because he was driving—and I had an apple martini. I liked that about him: he knew what I liked. We sat and looked at the menus, and as we did, he told me that I had some admirers. I asked him to explain. When I had excused myself to the bathroom, there were some guys a couple of tables over looking our way. They were talking in Spanish to each other, complimenting me on how beautiful I was. One guy commented on my nice legs. They must not have thought Dashad would understand them. He leaned over and replied in Spanish that he was a very lucky man, and thanked them. He said their faces were shocked, but they had apologized with smiles. Dashad didn't show signs of a jealous man. He was happy that he was with me, and I was happy that I was with him.

Just then, the owner of the restaurant came over to our table. Dashad stood up, they hugged, and then he introduced me. The short, Italian-looking gentleman kissed my hand and told me that I was beautiful. I thanked him, and he said that I was with a great guy. They talked for a while, and then he excused himself and went to the back of the restaurant. Ten minutes later, three waiters came out to our table with different appetizers. There was no room; the table was covered with an array of different appetizers, and they also brought out more drinks. This was love, and it made me even more proud to be with him that night. He was loved. He must be a good man, because people wanted to show their love, to make him feel special.

Everything was delicious, and yes I did take home a doggy bag. Dashad insisted that I try everything, even though I didn't have room in my stomach to try all that was given to us that night. Everything was just wonderful. We started back home. The music was so lively on the radio that we reminisced as each song came on, singing our favorite parts. We were home before we knew it. I hated for him to leave me. I wished we could be together always. *Maybe one day soon,* I thought. He walked me to my door and kissed me goodnight. Then he drove off. I stared out the door like a little puppy until he pulled off and was out of my sight.

As usual, I got right back to my routine: kids, store, and living. He was that exhale that you need every so often. We didn't really talk too much over the next couple of days, just checked in with each other. He had a lot to take care of, and so did I. I missed him, though. We finally made time to see each other, and once again we went out of town. This time I met his family. They loved me right from the start, I guess because he did. We arrived late in the morning, while everyone was moving and shaking trying to get ready for their day ahead. He had something to take care of with his cousin, so he left me there with the women. I have never felt so much love from someone that wasn't my family. They asked me a million times if I was OK or wanting anything. I ate breakfast there, and the food was delicious. It is good to taste real, good food that you didn't have to make. That was a treat for me. His favorite cousin, Latisha, had the most questions. I could tell they were close. She wanted to know it all.

"What are you?" she asked.

I didn't follow, so I looked at her so I could try to get a clue. "Sorry?" I asked her.

"What are you——Dominican? Puerto Rican? What are you mixed with?"

I just looked at her. "I'm black, not mixed with anything," I said.

She started laughing. "No, you look like you're mixed with something. It's your skin color. And your hair is so pretty," she explained.

"Thank you," I told her.

"I can tell my cousin really likes you," she offered.

"I like him too," I replied. I didn't want to pry and ask a lot of questions, but it was good to know that he was feeling me, too.

We went out to the park with the kids. They were all so cute. He came from a big family, so there were a lot of people to meet: big cousins, little cousins, husbands, and wives. I suddenly realized that he had been gone for three hours. Why would he leave me this long? What did he have to take care of that took this long? So I phoned him, but the cell was off. Latisha told me not to worry; he would be back. So I overlooked the time. Another hour passed, and I was wishing I had my truck, because I could have left. I was upset but didn't want his family to think I was a bitch. It was nice to spend time with them, but I could be home spending time with my own family. After the fifth hour, he called his cousin, telling him to bring me downstairs. I thanked the family for babysitting me and told them I had enjoyed meeting them. They said the same and to make sure I came back soon. I assured them I would.

As we took the elevator down, his cousin Blake offered an excuse for Dashad: "he had a lot of things to take care of, that's why he left you with us."

He must have been able to tell that I was upset. As soon as I saw Dashad, I knew he could tell also that I was bothered with him. I thanked Blake for walking me down, Dashad gave him a couple of dollars, and we left. I noticed that he always took care of everyone, and that they had great respect for him. As soon as we pulled off, I let him have it—in a nice way.

"Why did you leave me there so long, what were you doing?" I said.

"I was at the studio with my cousin," he replied. "Why, what happened?"

"Nothing, but I called you, and your phone was off."

"*Yes*—I was in the *studio*, recording," he said sarcastically.

"I knew it would be a minute, so I left you there. I knew you would be all right. Did you need anything?" He asked

"No."

"You ate, right? You had good time, right? You got to meet everyone, right? That's my family, not strangers. I knew you were good. I understand you were missing me, but don't be mad." He leaned over and gave me a kiss on my forehead. That was it, the end of that. I looked at him and just smiled.

"Where are we going now?" I asked.
"For a walk," he said.
"A walk? I have heels on—how far is this walk?"
"Five miles."
"I can't walk five miles with these heels on," I scolded.
"You're good you're with me; you won't even know you have on those heels."

We drove for a bit, and then he parked the car on a side street. We got out and walked to what looked like a highway. I was nervous: where were we going? Just then I looked up and noticed our surroundings. I was floored. Our date was to take a walk across the Brooklyn Bridge and back. That was the five-mile walk he was referring to. He was so original. I had never done it before. Most of the things he did with me, I had never done. I was amazed, and he noticed it and was happy. He extended his hand to me as we crossed the busy street and proceeded onto the bridge. There was a lot of traffic below us, cars racing to get to their destinations and people coming and going. Still, I felt like it was just us. As we walked across, and he started to tell me the story of the Brooklyn Bridge, my insides wanted to scream. The further that we walked onto the bridge, the tighter I gripped his hand. He asked me if I was afraid, and I told him I was afraid of heights. He assured me that nothing would happen to me while he was with me. I could trust him. I relaxed and trusted him. As I relaxed, I noticed the beautiful scenery, the powerful structure of the bridge, the gothic arches, and the water. I tuned out all the horns and noise from the cars below. It was wonderful. He went on talking about the bridge. I learned that its construction had begun in 1870, and that it was completed in May of 1883. We sat where Denzel Washington had been filmed, in some movie he was in. Before I knew it, we were on the other side.

Hello, Brooklyn. But we didn't stop there; we turned around. I had done it; I had crossed the bridge on foot. As we turned around to walk, I noticed people jogging or just walking like we were. Coming back over was delightful. Looking at the Manhattan skyline while the sun was starting to set reminded me of one of those pictures you see in barbershops or restaurant walls, of the skyline with the lights. It was so nice. We sat down and I told Dashad how happy I was to be with him. He had showed me so many things, and I thanked him. He said he just wanted to show me the world. We walked back over, still holding hands. We walked past older couples, taking their nightly stroll. *Would that be us?* I thought.

While he talked, my eyes were glued to this beautiful picture in 3-D, the lights bouncing off the water. The experience made me feel good all over. As we came to the end, he asked me what would make this the best date ever, and I replied "ice cream." He thought that was a great idea. We ate our ice cream cones at a local shop close to the bridge and then proceeded on to the highway. I didn't go home that night; I went back to Dashad's house. I was glad, because with the way I was feeling after that evening, we needed some privacy. I wanted to give him more of me, more than I had ever given before.

We got to his house. He hadn't even shut the door before he turned to me and told me, "Put your ass up in the air, I'll be there in a second."

Of course I agreed. I nodded my head and said OK, like I was a little girl swaying back and forth with my fingers in my mouth, just feeling so happy. I wanted him bad. I moved like he had paid me to do it. I did just what he said. I took my dress off and got up on the bed and spread my ass wide. I waited until he came in, which was about one minute. As soon as he came in, he smacked me on my ass. I turned my head to him and looked at him with a devilish grin. "I have been a bad girl," I said

"I know. I'm going to take care of it right now," he said.

He stuck his dick in me so far I could feel it in my stomach. He started off nice and slow. That's the kind of dick that drives you crazy. It was pure enjoyment. It was so intense. He climbed up on me like he was trying to mount a horse. That's right, I was a beautiful stallion. *Ride me, Daddy, ride on.* "It feels good, baby, huh?" I asked.

"Yes!" he said, short of breath. We went on in that position for a while, going hard with an occasional slap on my ass cheek to keep me jolted. He was loving it, I would look back from time to time and see the pleasure he was taking in me. Between the sheets, the passion between us was unbelievable.

Chapter Five

The Situation

Now that we had been dating for a few months, Dashad told me that it was time for him to interact with the children. He had seen them from time to time when he picked me up or dropped me off. But actually having a relationship, no, he did not. We started going out as a family, to dinner, movies, and amusement parks. He thought it would be good to start with Amir on a one-on-one basis. They both had a love for sports, so I knew they would have a lot in common. They went to a Philadelphia 76ers game; girls couldn't come. I guess it was a man thing. I could tell that the children were a little hesitant because of my last relationship, but they grew to know that Dashad was different. It was nice to have a family again, a complete family.

We didn't have to always go out; we could enjoy each other with the children. If we needed alone time, then we would go to his place, which we did two or three times a week. He was a part of the family. My mom and brothers loved him. He was a great man. I had also become part of his extended family. His cousin and I grew to be very close.

Then, just when I thought it couldn't get any better, I found out that Dashad had a woman.

Leah and Monique called me on three-way, and I could tell something was wrong. I had known them too long not to notice; they just didn't sound happy.

"What's up?" I questioned.

"Can you talk?" asked Leah.

"Yeah, what's going on?" I demanded. "Is everything OK?"

"I have some bad news to tell you about D," said Leah.

My heart stopped. I couldn't move. My mind was racing, thinking all kinds of things.

"Hello?" questioned Mo.

"Isis?" Leah shouted.

"What happened?" You could hear distress in my voice.

"No, nothing like that. He's OK," Leah informed me.

"For now," Monique added.

"Can you please just tell me? I'm going crazy over here."

Leah began the story, telling me how she was over at Bryan's having some down time. Bryan's phone was blowing up, ringing every two minutes until Leah told him to answer it. She said she could tell that he didn't want to, but she wanted to see what the fuss was all about. It was Dashad's girl, looking for him. He was with me. She said the girl was crying and saying that she knew he was messing around. She asked Bryan if he knew about it. Of course he lied, because that's the code. Anyway, he had to tell Leah what was going on because she had heard some on the conversation. He asked her not to tell me because she didn't know the whole situation, but she let him know that I was her girl and I had a right to know. To her surprise, he let her in on his secret. He also had a woman. She said after he told her that she just got up and left.

My mind was still stuck. I didn't understand anything that she was saying. How could he have a woman? Where had she been all of these months? Why would he do this to me and my family? I had so many questions, and the only way they would get answered was by calling D myself.

"Hello?" said Monique.

"I will call you guys back," I replied.

"Wait!" demanded Leah.

"For what?" I questioned.

"Just calm down before you call him, that's all."

"OK." I hung up. I just wanted to talk to him. "We have been husband and wife in the bedroom," I wanted to tell him. "I have let you explore every part of me. I let you in. You have made a home within my family." I started to dial. The phone rang once, and then went to voice mail. I called again, and it did the same. This time I left a message telling him to call me; I had to talk to him. That was the first time I had called and left a message. My mind was racing, thinking *why would he do this to me?* I only loved and cared for him. He was with her now, arguing.

Who was she? What did she look like? How could he pull this off? I had been with his family and friends. How could he account for all the nights he wasn't home? He had his own place, and I had keys to the door. Something wasn't right. Just then, my phone rang back. I said hello, then it hung up. It was Dashad. I tried to return the call, but it went straight to voice mail.

I didn't know what to do. I called Monique back so we could talk. Leah was upset about her own situation, and I needed to talk to someone with a clear mind.

I talked to Monique for about an hour. I was a little bit better, but not completely. She told me to let him tell his side of the story: "you don't know what's going on, so relax and just wait to talk to him." She didn't think I should overreact before I found out all the facts. I thanked her because I couldn't talk to anyone about this. It was too embarrassing. She assured me that, no matter what, I would be fine. She always knew what to say. She was a great friend.

It was killing me, so I called his cousin in New York. I wanted to know if she knew anything. I was glad that I called her: I found out what I needed to know. The woman was the mother of the last child that he had. She had called Latisha asking if there was anyone in the family named Isis. I asked her why she hadn't told me that her cousin was with someone. She informed me that was his place to tell me. She told me that he did love me and wanted to be with me, but he had a child by her. Once again, I felt a little better, but not completely. I still needed to talk with him.

Two days passed—I had never gone that long without talking to him—before he called me. He told me he wanted to meet me. We met at a diner midway between us. I got there first. I went inside, got a table, and ordered myself some coffee. Shortly after, he came in. He ordered tea. After the lady left the table, he opened his mouth. "I'm sorry that all of this happened," he said. "I never wanted to hurt you in any way."

I just sat there quiet. I wanted to know everything. If I interrupted, that might mess up the flow of the conversation.

"Are you all right?" he asked.

"What do you think?" I said sarcastically. "I finally find a man that everyone in my family loves, that is perfect for me, and come to find out he has a relationship with another woman. I would say that I am not all right."

"Again, I am sorry."

"Sorry for getting caught?" I interrupted. "How can you do this to me? I've been nothing but great to you."

"You have. I just didn't know how to tell you."

"Umm . . . 'I am in a relationship with someone?' That was easy, right? I've been intimate with you like you were my husband. Is everything you told me a lie?"

"Wait a minute; what I feel for you will never change. I just have a situation."

"You think?"

"All right, I know you're upset, but calm down. You have nothing to do with her."

My heart just dropped. "What do you mean by that?"

"I want to be with you, but she has my child. I don't want another man around her. If she knew of you, she would be spiteful and keep my daughter away from me. You of all people know that I love my children."

"You have been fighting with her?"

"Why do you ask that?"

"You have a bite mark on your arm."

He looked down and then replied, "It got a little rough, but everything is OK now."

"You hit her!"

"No, just had to duck and dodge a few things."

I stared at him in amazement as he described what he had been going through. Could this really be my life?

"I don't want to lose you. I need for you to understand what I'm up against here."

"You want to have your cake and eat it, too."

"No, I want to be happy. You make me happy. She has nothing to do with you, and you have nothing to do with her. Have you been affected in anyway until now?"

"No."

"She had been going through my phone. I call you before I go in the house, and she had noticed over a period of time that it was the same number. She called your phone and heard your recording."

"In the house? So you don't live at the house I have keys to?"

"Yes, I live there. But I also own the house that my family lives in."

"Your family?" I said in a displeased tone.

"Yes, my family."

"I don't know what you want me to do, here."

"Nothing has changed."

"Oh, but it has. I have to go. This is too much."

I got my things and headed to the car. I didn't even look back. I just left. I was so hurt. *Why me?* I thought. I was just about to get in the car when he touched my shoulder.

"Please wait."

"This is a first for me with this. I don't know what to say, but I know I don't want you to go."

"Why should I stay, to be the other woman?"

"It wouldn't be like that, and you know it. I have respect for you, you know I do."

I did love him, and I wanted to be with him. I was happy, and while I had been with him it hadn't ever been a problem. I hadn't even known about her. She wasn't an issue. I could understand how he looked at the situation with his daughter being around another man. People were crazy out there; you never knew. I just stood there looking at him.

"It's still me, the same person. Please. I don't want to lose you."

"I would miss you terribly, too."

He smiled and hugged me. He held onto me so tight. When he kissed me I felt that he was sorry for hurting me. I just told him that his worlds should never cross.

He assured me that they wouldn't. We sat in the car and talked for about an hour, then I went back home. I guess you can say he went back home, too.

On the drive home, I was thinking *Am I crazy, desperate, that I still want to be with him?* No, I decided, I was in love, and I believed him. I did know some women could be spiteful. I just chalked it up to her. He was obligated to her, because he had a child with her. He wanted to be with *me* just for me. I wouldn't be affected.

After that incident, he called me a lot more than usual, letting me know his whereabouts. He made me feel comfortable, so I didn't really think of our situation much. I would never bump into her; we lived an hour away from each other. I pushed it to the back of my mind and was hoping no one on my side would learn of this, my little secret.

I called Mo and Leah and let them know that I had spoken with him. The funny thing is that Bryan had had a similar story for Leah. Had we been duped? It didn't matter. I believed him and wanted to stick it out.

Leah had decided the same. Monique informed us that she wasn't happy with our decisions and would be coming to town next week. I was so happy that she was coming. I needed some support.

Monique lived in Los Angeles, California. She was a big-time writer and editor for her own magazine, *Renaissance Woman*. She had to meet with some people from the East Coast to talk about marketing for the magazine out here. She was going bicoastal. She would only be in town for three days, but that was perfect. She hasn't visited for two years; on holidays, she usually went to visit her family in Dallas. Right now, with this mess going on, I needed her. We were like two peas in a pod. I had to plan a party at the restaurant so we could all get together.

I called my mother and asked her to put a sign up informing customers that on Sunday the restaurant would be closed. If any customers were to ask why, she was to tell them it had been rented out for a party. I was so excited that she was coming; I called D and let him know. He said he would be there. Of course Leah and Bryan would be there, and our families, too. I had Leah call some of her friends from school to attend the party. This was wonderful: I would be busy planning the party, and it would take my mind off of what was going on.

Nothing had really changed; things remained the same as before. Everything was swept under the rug. The next time we made love, I had insisted that he wear protection. He wasn't happy, but he understood why I felt that way. I should not have assumed he was sleeping only with me just because I was sleeping only with him. You must protect yourself at all times.

That week we went to New York again to spend some quality time together and visit his family. This time he took me to Justin's—P. Diddy's restaurant—to eat. The décor was nice, and the staff was friendly. It was crowded, but D worked his magic; he slid the hostess—who, I might add, was staring at him a little too much—a twenty dollar bill to seat us next. It was nice; it's always nice to be in a crowd of nicely dressed people wanting to have a good time. The mood was perfect. There was music while we were eating, a DJ in the corner playing old-school hip hop beats. We were so pleased with the DJ that we asked the hostess if he had CDs to sell. She gave us a Web site where we could order them. Dinner was great. I had the popcorn shrimp as an appetizer, and the beef ribs smothered in gravy. It was delicious; I wanted to go back and speak with the chef. We told our waitress to inform the chef that the food was great. Before we left, he came to the door of the kitchen, waved, and mouthed thank you. We left stuffed and leaning—the drinks were great too. He looked at me and told me that he had never been there with her; he would only take me to new places. I did appreciate that, but why did he even have to bring her up? Was he thinking about her, or was he still really sorry and just wanting me to know? It didn't matter; I didn't want to spoil the mood. That night he stayed at my house. This time we didn't make love, we just slept. That felt just as good, him holding me all night.

We got up to get breakfast going, and when the children came downstairs, they were happy to see that Dashad was there. Everybody was bombarding him with questions and trying to tell him new things that had happened in their lives. It was great. As I stood there looking at how happy the children were, I let it all go. I didn't care anymore. That was for him to deal with.

I got the kids off, and Dashad left shortly after to take care of his business. Today was a big day: I had to get Mo from the airport. I was so excited. I really missed her. I got there just in time, as the plane was letting its passengers off. Just then I saw her, looking so Hollywood. She noticed me at the same time.

"Hey!" she shouted.

"Hey!" I shouted back. I went over to hug her. People were looking at us, but we didn't care. We missed each other. We were acting like Celie and Nettie, like we had been reunited after a long time.

"What's up? You look good," I told her.

"No, you look good. I hope to look like you once I have my babies."

"Shut up."

We hugged again. I was so glad to see her. We went to get her bags—of which, I might add, she had too many for a three-day stay—and some nice, cute gentlemen offered to assist us. One of them offered Mo his number once we got to the car.

She was a stunning woman with all the right measurements. She was tall, with an *America's Next Top Model* figure. She kind of looked like Tyra Banks.

We got to the restaurant to see my mom and my brother. Monique loved my mom's sweet potato pie and potato salad. We pulled up to the restaurant and went in. She went into the door first, and I followed as we laughed and talked about old times. "Surprise!" a group of Mo's family and friends yelled. It was perfect: they scared the shit out of her. I laughed forever. She was happy to see everyone. She told me, "You're a trip. I didn't suspect anything. Thank you." She had thought we were going to get together with everyone the last day she was here.

"I am one of your many friends that can hold a secret," I replied. Everyone crowded her, welcoming her home. A lot of people showed up. Dashad and Bryan even came, which was perfect. I wanted her to meet him. We celebrated, laughing, loving, drinking, and dancing horribly. It was perfect. I know she wouldn't have time to see everybody, so why not get everyone in one place to share a good time and good food? We had a great time, Bryan and Leah seemed just like Dashad and me, everything pushed under the rug. Monique made her way back around the room to our table. I introduced Dashad and Bryan, and everyone said their hellos. "Did you get to eat anything?" I asked.

"Girl, you know what I ate already," she said, smiling. She was referring to my mom's pie and potato salad. This was a big night for me—Monique coming home and Dashad meeting my extended family. He did a great job. He was so well-mannered; he knew the right things to say. My cousin Aurora was even there and she liked him. It was good connecting with her again. She had moved down south with James, and they had just come back up north. I enjoyed myself as all hard-working women should. I got to see my godchildren; they were growing up so fast. The DJ livened up the party, playing Frankie Beverly and Maze's "Before I let go." Everyone got up and formed lines on the floor and began doing the cupid shuffle. The night was perfect.

I was a little too intoxicated that night, so I asked my mother if she could go home with the kids and Monique. Of course she agreed; she wanted to ask Mo some questions about LA. My mom loved Monique. I informed Dashad that we were getting a room once my mother agreed, and I excused myself from the party. My excuse was that I drank too much. That is never a bad thing at a party, unless you throw up in front of everyone, anyway everyone understood. Perfect, now I could have him all to myself. He looked so nice. The more I drank, the more he made me hot. We didn't go far, just down the road to the Doubletree Hotel. I love the rooms: their pillows and beds are so soft. I asked Dashad to get my bag out of the back of the truck. He went and paid for the room, then got it. Once he picked it up, he saw that it was heavy.

"What's in here?" he asked.

"Some tricks and treats." He just smiled as he opened the door to the room. As I walked past him, I gave a seductive kiss, grabbed the bag, and said, "I'll be back in five minutes. Get comfortable, OK?"

I had been planning this night for a week. I was prepared. I had everything in that bag. What I love about the suites at our hotel was that they had two complete divided rooms, a living room area, and a bedroom area with a sink in the room. The bathroom just had a toilet and shower. As he sat in the living area of the suite, I got dressed. When I say I had everything in that bag, I meant everything:

Four different outfits

Two pair of shoes—that went with all four outfits

One bottle of Hennessy VSOP and one bottle of Jose Cuervo pre-made margaritas

Pepsi and bottled water.

Baby oil gel

Phillies

Scented candles—vanilla, sweet and clean

Small CD boom box

Condoms—the gold and black ones

The sexy mix CDs I'd been making all week

One bottle of caramel sundae syrup

I lit the candles first, before getting dressed; they provided some of the mood. I hooked the CD player up in the corner of the room and placed the condoms on the bedside table. I came out into the living room area with his drink, VSOP and Pepsi in a separate cup. He was very surprised, and now he knew it was going to be a show. I made myself a drink, too, but kept it in the bathroom so I could sip on it. I then got dressed. My first outfit made me look like a goddess, thanks to Amy at Victoria's Secret. She had helped me with everything. I only had on mascara, piña colada body splash, and a baby blue cotton lace teddy. It accentuated my curves.

I put my hair in two ponytails with matching baby blue ribbons and put on my sexy college-girl glasses. I wore three-inch white stilettos. I didn't want to fall during my performance. I had planned to start off with the CD with the best of both worlds, Jay-Z and R. Kelly's 'Fiesta. Latisha had told me that was one of Dashad's favorite songs. He was in for a treat because I was feeling right. I had been drinking shots of Jose Cuervo and margaritas all night, celebrating with my family and friends.

Everyone loved Dashad. I was feeling real sexy. The last time we had made love, I wasn't really into it. But I had since forgiven him, so this was the makeup sex.

I came into the room, and he looked up and froze, literally, just staring at me. I smiled. He told me to come sit beside him. I sat down and placed the caramel syrup on the table. He kissed me on my forehead and got up. He walked around the table in front of the couch, not looking away from me at all, and then he bent down and took my shoes off and started rubbing my feet. He told me I looked beautiful. He was treating me exactly how I was feeling, like a goddess. We talked about my family while he rubbed my feet. He liked everyone. I was glad because that was important to me, not just that he got along with the children, but my extended family as well. I didn't want him to stop, but I had to get ready for my show. I told him to sit down; he was already in his Ralph Lauren boxers looking like my sexy king. I got up, put my shoes back on, and went into the other room and turned the CD on. I guess that was our little thing: we spoke through words of songs that we liked. I could see his face when he heard his song. Pure delight.

I walked over to him like the sexy feline that I was, turned around slowly, and bent over and spread my ass. I saw his reflection through the television, and I almost laughed because he sat up so fast to get a closer look. He made me feel so sexy. He liked my nice round hips as I was rolling them in his face; he grabbed a hold and slowly caressed my oily booty. I had him. He was pleased. I was popping my ass up and down. I couldn't believe it myself—it was the tequila, blame it on the alcohol. Occasionally I would turn around, but he was loving the ass action he was getting. The fast tempo had me bouncing. My arms were swaying seductively and caressing my D-cup breasts. The song ended, but I was prepared. There were seventeen songs on that CD, and the next one was Jay-Z's "The Bounce"—another bouncing and shaking song. It was a nice selection of songs: Trick Daddy and Jaheim's "Fucking tonight," 50 Cent's "Candy Shop," Ludacris's "Money Maker," and Jaheim's "Slow it down some," to name a few. He loved his show. Before long he grabbed my hand and led me into the bedroom.

We were so deep in our freak we didn't even notice that the candle next to us was on fire. The smoke detector went off, breaking our connection. It was a loud searing sound. I hadn't taken the bamboo rope wrapped around the candle off, so the candle burned down and the rope caught fire. I couldn't believe we hadn't seen it; the whole thing was on fire. *We were busy.* He got up and got some water and a towel. He contained it fast. Just then the phone rang, it was the front desk. They wanted to know if everything was all right. D explained to them that we'd had a candle lit, but that we had put it out. I guess they have sensors in each room so they don't have to evacuate the building for nothing. While D cleaned up the mess, I went into the bathroom and refreshed myself. This time I came out in a sheer black teddy with black stilettos and a small whip with thin leather tassels. I stood in the door and gently smacked my leg to get his attention. When he noticed me, I walked over and pushed him on the bed. I straddled him and rode him like he was a beautiful black stallion. Every now and then, he would use the leather tassel to give me a giddy up.

The next day, I didn't even remember going to sleep. I just woke up with a migraine the size of Texas. He got me some Tylenol and OJ. I just wanted to go home; I felt horrible. I had overdone it. I was glad that I didn't throw up.

I called my mom to see what everyone was doing, and they were all having breakfast. I told her we were coming. Once everyone saw me, they knew I'd had too much to drink. I grabbed a pancake and went to my room. Dashad stayed in the kitchen with everyone, and then checked on me before he left. I was OK; I just needed more sleep, I guess.

It was good that I didn't have to be the tour guide, because Monique had her meetings. I had promised the kids that we would go to the funplex, however. After my nap, I got dressed, and we were on our way. The kids had so much fun: they got on the bumper cars, played in the ball room, and batted in the cages. Once we got home, I checked in with Dashad, but there was no answer. After her meeting, Monique went to visit her grandmother. Nya and I stretched out in my bed watching Dora cartoons.

The next night, Dashad had plans for all of us to go out: me, Monique, and her friend Jamie. He took us to a comedy spot on South Street, The Laugh House. Of course, we were late, so when we walked in, the comedian commented that we looked lovely—but we were late. We sat in the back so he wouldn't continue to snap on us all night. We ordered drinks and got into the show. It was nice for all of us to be out and enjoying each other's company. I was happy that Dashad had made such a good impression with Monique. The comedian was funny. Some guy I had never seen before came to the table and whispered to Dashad. He thanked him, and then the guy left. I wanted to be nosy, but I just let it be. He would tell me; he knew I wanted to know. The guy was an employee of the Laugh House. He had gotten the news that Jill Scott was across the street at some lounge. She had performed in the city that night and was over there. The guy gave Dashad a pass so that we could go over there and meet her. It was a night to remember.

Before long Monique, had to go back to LA. I was going to miss her. It seemed like her trip had ended too soon. Dashad and I took her to the airport.

Chapter Six

Keep Your Hands to Yourself

Dashad called me early the next morning. I was already at the restaurant. I was busy handling orders and returning calls to customers who wanted to book us for their parties. I explained to him I would call him back. He insisted that I talk, but I repeated myself and told him I had to call him back. I had been noticing that he was becoming very demanding and sometimes even rude. I understood that I was his woman, but he didn't own me. Dashad begged to differ. Earlier that week, he had hired a nanny. He wanted someone to be there all the time so when he needed me it wasn't an issue to get away.

That night, we got into a heated argument. We had never really had an argument: we had disagreed, but never had a full-blown argument. He wanted me to come see him, but I couldn't. I had people that I needed to meet the next morning. I had to be well-rested. I had been ignoring a lot lately and putting things off on my mother and brother. I had to play my part. It was my place. I hung up on him; I wasn't going to continue to argue. He didn't even call me back that night. But this argument wasn't like a normal one; it went on for a week. I didn't know what the hell was going on, but we were not feeling each other that whole week. I was sad, but I hadn't done anything wrong to him.

I phoned Leah to see if she had any idea why he was that way. She told me he had lost ten thousand dollars in Atlantic City last week. Bryan had told her. Now I understood: when he'd lost the money, he had wanted me to come down there and be with him, to comfort him, but I couldn't because I had to work. I chatted with Leah for a bit, and then called him again. I should have given him time to cool off—that was lot of money.

"Hey, babe," I said in a gentle voice.

"What's up?" he asked, like he was talking-to one of his boys.
"I just wanted to see if you were OK."
"You coming to see me?" he asked.
"I didn't plan on it."
"Why?"
"I need to stay close to home. A lot is going on, and I need to be here."

He just hung up the phone. I didn't call back, either. The hell with him: no one told him to go down there and lose all that money. What a waste. I did feel bad, so I called him the next day to tell him I was coming down. He told me he was "doing stuff with my family."

"What, you guys are a family now?" I questioned. "Fuck you and your family."

Then I hung up. I couldn't believe he had just said that shit to me, but I shouldn't have said that, either. I didn't mean his child, I meant *her*. I went about my day—mind you, with a little attitude—but it is what it is. I enjoyed myself, relaxing and doing little household things that needed to be done.

A few hours later, Dashad called me and asked me if I still was coming down there. I thought he was bipolar or something. I didn't even bring it up what he had said earlier; instead I was trying to be the bigger person. I forgot all about it, but he didn't. I told him to give me an hour to get the kids situated.

I got down there and he met me at the house; we pulled up at about the same time. I was excited to see him, but worried about his attitude. When we got to the door, I did sense something, but just thought he was not himself due to the money he had lost. He would win it back, that I was sure of.

He opened the door and kissed me and told me to go put my ass is the air. I did just that, and he came into the room before I got onto the bed. He had a Heineken beer in his hand, which was odd; that really wasn't his choice of drink. One of his hands was behind his back. Now he didn't look like himself. He was calm, though, so I still didn't know what to think. He came closer and said, "Now what was that you were saying earlier?"

"What?" I asked. I didn't understand, I was in sexy mode.

"What you said to me earlier." He then pulled a wire hanger from behind his back and smacked me on my leg with it. I jumped up and told him to stop. It stung something awful. He hit me again, this time lashing at my arms. I tried to block him, but it was just continuous. I started to cry, begging him to stop. He told me I needed to be taught a lesson. I screamed, "All I ever did was love you! Why would you do this to me?" I just kept crying, wanting it to be over. After every hit from the hanger, he would say something: "Stay still," "Oh I thought you were tough," "You've never been loved like this before, not even from your parents." He would even kiss my mouth periodically in between the hits. I was in hell, didn't know when this horror would stop. I was jumping all around the room trying to get free of him, but he just kept hitting me. He gave me fourteen lashes with that hanger, to be exact. The last one was across my back that hurt the worst. I think he saw that, and that was it. I sat naked, balled up on the bed, crying my eyes out. I was thinking I was going to kill him when I got the chance. He must have read that on my face, because he went into the laundry room where he kept his shotgun, came back in the bedroom, and ejected the bullets out of the gun right in front of me. He was looking right at me, letting me know that he was smarter than me. He then told me if I were to leave his house he would come to my house and beat me in front of my children. Then he told me to get into the bath; it would help the welts. *Who was this man?* He went on to mumble that he had left what he was doing to come straighten me out. He left the room, and then I heard the front door close hard. I didn't move. I was scared to death. Never in my wildest dreams would I have thought that was going to go down. I then heard the car pull off out of the driveway. I sat in that very same spot and cried all night. I noticed that the sun was coming up when I started to get tired. I knew that he was gone and wasn't coming back. He was over there with her. I fell asleep. When I woke, it was about nine in the morning. I thought it had been a dream, until I felt every lash on my body. I got up and looked at myself. It was horrible. I had a contusion on my thigh, and thick red welts everywhere. Why would he do this to me? I began to cry again, looking at my body. How could I hide this? What would my family do if they saw this? My children? I just became numb. I couldn't cry anymore. I just lay down in the bed.

Not long afterwards, Dashad came back. I heard the car pull up, then the front door. I heard the cabinet and refrigerator open and close, and then he came in the room with some water. He looked at me, but I wouldn't look at him. He asked me if I was all right, but still no response from me. He sat down on the bed and rubbed my head.

"I'm sorry, but you will never talk to me again like that, *ever!*"

Then he got into the bed and lay down beside me. I hated him. I wanted to stab him in the heart. How can you beat someone then hours later want to cuddle? He wanted me, but I didn't respond to his touch. He went under the covers and began having his way with me, but I still did not respond. I didn't want him touching me at all, but I was scared that he would hit me some more, so I just lay there. After about five or ten minutes down there, he saw that it wasn't going to work, so he climbed onto me. He had to be disgusted, because it was like he was having sex with a dead person. I didn't move, not even a little bit. After he was done, I just lay there, still in shock at what my life had become. He ran some water in the tub for me and tried to help me with the pain by offering Tylenol. I took the pills and got into the tub and closed the door. I didn't want to talk to him or look at him. I wanted to know when he was going to let me leave. As I thought about it some more, I started to cry. I was a good person. Why would this happen to me?

He ordered lunch from a local pizzeria. I didn't eat. I didn't talk, either. I just wanted to go home. So I asked, "Can I go now?"

"You want to go home?" he asked me.

"Yes."

"How about you stay with me another night? I have already called your mother and asked her to tend to the children," he explained.

I didn't want to, but I stayed another night. I didn't know why he wanted to be around me. We didn't speak at all. I just watched television in the bedroom, while he watched in the living room. Every once in a while, he would check on me. The welts were still very visible on my legs, arms, and back. He left and went out for a minute, thoughtfully taking my cell with him so I couldn't call anyone. Who would I tell that he had done this to me? I was so embarrassed. I looked everywhere in the house for my purse, but I couldn't find it. I guess he took that, too.

He came back from the store with some Aveeno oatmeal bath so that I could soak in it and soothe my skin. The contusion was still rather large. After I got out of the tub again, I took three Tylenol and went to sleep.

I awoke the next morning to find that he had cooked breakfast. I still didn't have an appetite. I wanted to leave. I explained to him I was ready to go. Surprisingly, he told me that I could. I asked for my bag, and he went towards the microwave, opened it up, and grabbed my bag out of it. I never would have looked in there. I couldn't get out the door fast enough. I was rushing, I forgot my cell phone. I didn't care, either. I wasn't going back.

I finally got home, and no one was there. What a relief. I got into my own tub and soaked some more, then went through my closet trying to find clothes that would cover my body.

I didn't talk to Dashad for many days after that. I would not accept his calls. He sent flowers every day, saying how sorry he was. That weekend, he showed up unannounced at my home, knocking on the door. I called his cell and told him I didn't feel like company. He pleaded with me to open the door. He stood out there for three hours. I didn't care. My next door neighbor phoned me, letting me know there was a man sitting outside on my walkway. I explained to her that he was on timeout, and she chuckled and said, "You got to teach them." He put my phone in the mailbox, and then he finally left. I knew he was mad, but why would I let him in here? I didn't trust him anymore. *He beat me with a wire hanger.* I wasn't his child, I was his woman.

I prayed a lot about what happened that day, and I slowly got better. You can never really get over something like that, but I learned to put it in a box and never open it again. It helped, it really did. I had to mentally heal myself. I had to forgive him, but I wasn't ready to yet.

The next time he came back, he waited until I came out the house and approached me.

"Can I *please* talk to you?" he asked.

"What, Dashad?"

"Please, I'm sorry. I don't know what got into me. I'm sorry. I need you."

"For what, to take your shit out on me? Leave me alone, please."

"I can't," he said.

When he said that, I turned around.

"What?" I asked.

"I can't leave you alone. Can we please go inside and talk?"

I agreed. We sat in the kitchen on separate sides of the kitchen table. I chose the kitchen so that if he had any ideas, he would be a dead man, leaving here in a body bag. He pleaded with me and expressed how sorry he was. He wouldn't do it again. After three hours about his childhood, the horrors of his dad hitting his mom and their constant fighting, I forgave him. He seemed like he had remorse for what he had done. If God could forgive him, I could, too.

Things with us went back to normal fast. Another situation swept under the rug. Months went by, and not an argument between us. We were both in our glory, according to our Libra horoscope: we were in a Libra moon. Dashad and I have birthdays ten days apart. I got him a leather recliner for his birthday, one that folded all the way out so he could sleep comfortable in the chair, which is where he usually falls asleep, after watching television. The History Channel and CNN were his favorite programs to watch. He was delighted that I had put so much thought into his gift. It was something he needed, and every man wants to have his own chair.

My birthday rolled around, and he kept things a surprise, I had a nice dinner with my family and got many gifts. Dashad couldn't make it; he had business he had to take care of, so I was to meet him at his house after dinner with my family.

I got to his house around nine that night. He wasn't there, and I had forgotten my key. I had taken it off of my key chain a while ago when I thought I was done with him. I had to sit for an hour, and on top of that my cell phone had died. My birthday was turning out to be a mess. He finally showed up, saying he thought something had happened to me because I wasn't answering my cell or the house phone. I let him know I had forgotten my key and that my phone had died. Once he saw that I was all right, he smiled and said, "Happy Birthday!"

"Thank you."

We went inside and sat down, and I told him all about dinner and the lovely gifts that I had gotten from my family. He apologized for not attending, and I said it was OK. He told me he didn't really have a lot of time to go get me anything, but he did get me something. He said it was in the back. I walked to the back room and saw a long white box. The type of box Patti Labelle would get before a show. I opened up the box, and it was roses. They were so beautiful, in full bloom with long stems. The roses had glitter on them; they were just so pretty. I kissed him and said thank you. He knew how much I loved flowers. We went back into the living room to get comfortable. He kept apologizing for not being able to get me anything. He said he should have planned earlier for this, but he had some things to take care of. I didn't care. We were chilling, and birthdays are for the children anyway. I was just glad that we were over the bad shit that has happened to us over the last couple of months. He did get us a bottle of Rosé Moët to toast to my birthday. We laughed and drank the champagne, and then I excused myself to the bathroom. A little too much of the bubbly. I looked over at my Diva roses, smiled, and went into the bathroom. I came back and sat back on the couch next to D, and noticed a teal box with silver ribbon wrapped around it on the table. That was not there when we came in the house. I looked at him and smiled. He insisted that I open it. I did, and found a set of princess-cut diamond stud earrings from Tiffany's. I was so excited. He took the box from me, I removed my earrings that I had on, and he put the studs in my ears. He told me that he didn't ever want me to take them off. I agreed. I also asked him why he had acted like he didn't get me anything. He really wanted it to be a surprise. We continued to drink—another bottle of Moët—and now I was really good. I had to go to the bathroom again. This time, when I came out, all the lights were off. *Oh, it's time to be sexy*, I thought. D wasn't in the living room; he was in the kitchen. Just then, I looked over and saw a light in all of the darkness. He came around the corner with a cake and candles on it, singing happy birthday. I was floored, he really had me fooled. I just smiled as he sang the chorus. He sat the cake down in front of me, and I blew the candles out. He turned the lights back on, and my cheeks were stuck. I was so elated. He was too much. This was so sweet. He had wanted me all to himself on my birthday. It was really special. The cake was a three-layer vanilla cake with banana filling, and strawberry filling, and butter cream icing—the best cake I had ever tasted in my life. We sat and ate the cake. I wanted to eat another piece, but didn't want to seem greedy. *Oh hell*, I thought, *it's my day*. I had another. That was three pieces of cake in one day. Can you say sugar rush? The evening was perfect; we didn't even make love that night. We sat up and talked, listening to Jaheim's new CD. The lighting was perfect, the music was right, the mood was delightful. I felt in love with him all over again, which is what he was going for. We needed a new start. So I thought.

That following week, he went to visit his family in New York. He insisted that I drive up, so I did. They haven't seen us in a while, so everyone was happy to see us. I loved his family; they were real down-to-earth people who accepted you for who you were and nothing else. You could be yourself and not have to worry.

One of his cousins had just come home, so we had more celebrating to do. As always, we split up. He went with the boy cousins and I stayed with the aunts and girl cousins. They cooked, and I ate. I loved the mixture of island blends. I was thinking about incorporating that into my menu at Meek's. It was getting late, and a lot of the family was leaving. I helped one of his cousins and her children downstairs so that she could get a cab home. I also wanted to see what D was doing. He told me he was ready to go, and for me to get my things. I went back upstairs and said my see-you-laters. I came right back down. Dashad was waiting in his car for me. One of his cousins was in the backseat. I got in, and we drove off. We pulled up shortly to some building, and D went inside.

All of a sudden, D came back out of the building, and jumped into the car, and pulled off. He was upset about something, but wouldn't answer me as I asked him what was wrong. He was doing ninety miles an hour down narrow streets, and I was truly scared. I kept asking him over and over to slow down, but he just kept ignoring me. His cousin was hollering for him to slow down, but he ignored us. He went through a red light. I thought we were going to die. We could not see the oncoming traffic; there could have been a car or cars that we would have collided into. Now I was hysterical, hollering for him to stop right now. He turned to me with a long-necked Hennessey bottle in his hand and tapped me on my forehead hard enough for me to turn forward, strap on my seatbelt, and just pray I would make it home to my babies. Dashad had lost his mind, and his cousin couldn't believe what was going on. He tried to plead with him and told him to think of his children. I think that worked, because at the next stoplight, he stopped. His cousin asked me if I was OK, but I never answered. I just sat there, still, praying that I would get home and wondering *why is this happening to me*? The light changed, and he took off again. His cousin insisted that D let him out of the car. Immediately, he slowed down. The car stopped and Dashad got out. His cousin followed. I just sat there in amazement. They both got into the car, and Dashad looked at me and said, "I'm sorry." I never turned to look in his face to see if he was sincere. I wanted to get away from that man. He was truly crazy.

Shortly after that, we pulled up to his aunt's building and he jumped out of the car, telling me to get into the driver's seat. I just sat there. His cousin asked me again if I was OK, and I told him yes. He really hadn't hit me hard, but what if it had broken on my face and cut me? I was sitting there sad, upset and not knowing what to do. His cousin said that he had gotten robbed in the building. That was why he was upset. I asked why we were here, and he said, "So he can get some heat." He was going back. Just then I saw Dashad with an object wrapped in a towel. I grabbed my bag and jumped out of the car. He saw me take off, ran to the car, put the object on the seat, and came after me. He had grabbed my bag trying to get to me. I let it go spilling all over the playground. He finally caught me. I was holding onto the metal fence for dear life. He kept insisting that I leave with him now, and he continued pulling on me. I wouldn't budge. This went on for about five minutes, and he ripped my jacket off of me and tore my shirt. I was devastated. I was in the middle of this playground fighting for my life. I was crying and screaming. His cousin came over to him and asked him what he was doing. He told him to leave me alone. Dashad ignored him. The cousin said he didn't want to be a part of this; he was leaving. I begged him not to go. If there weren't any witnesses, he could kill me. He had truly gone mad. Just then a woman opened up her window and shouted for him to let go of me. Of course, he told her to mind her own business. She said she was calling the police. He held me with one hand and pointed to the lady with the other, and then he counted the number floors and told her someone would be up to see her. She immediately withdrew her body back from the window and closed it. But now other people were wondering what was going on, so they were opening up their windows telling him to leave me alone. I saw a cop car, and I knew it would be over soon. He held onto me until the police officers, one man and one woman were fifty yards away from us. Then he let me go and went off running. I started running in the other direction. The lady officer kept calling me, telling to wait, but they went after Dashad. I never turned back; I just kept running up the block. My mind was racing, trying to think what I could do and where could I go.

 I remembered that Chrishonda, one of Dashad's cousins, had moved up the block to her grandmother's. She was having problems with her mother about her baby father. I called her and explained everything to her and asked her to meet me downstairs at her building. I got there as she was just getting off the elevator. I was so relieved to see her. She looked at me in shock. My clothes were ripped up, my hair was all messed up, and I was crying hysterically. We went upstairs to her grandmother's apartment. I explained what had happened and asked her if she would make me leave if he found me. She said no. She gave me another shirt and tried to calm me down, but she was as upset as I was. She didn't know what to think; she had never even heard of him losing his temper. I guess I knew her cousin a little more than she did. We sat for awhile and tried to come up with a plan to get me home. I had driven up there, so I would just have to wait until the coast was clear. Chrishonda called down to Dashad's aunt's house to see if he was there and what had happened with the police. His aunt didn't even know what she was talking about, but she did let her know that his car was no longer out back, but my truck still was. I explained to her that my bag was still at the playground and asked her to walk me down there so I could get my keys and go home. We walked down the block; everything was quiet. No one was out, and I thought my disastrous night was over. *Not quite yet.* We heard a man's voice exclaim, "Right there!" and all of a sudden we saw D and two men running up the block. He chased me around the parked cars, telling me I could have gotten him killed. As we were running around the car, I noticed that he had my keys in his hand. I told him I just wanted to go home; I wanted my keys. Chrishonda was screaming: "Cousin, cousin, what are you doing? Just let her go home!"

He looked at me and said, "Fuck you," and threw my keys at me. He then went down the block, and we went back to her house. She said she thought that we needed to get her boyfriend to walk us to my car; I think even she was afraid. He met us in front of the building. She explained what was going on. They walked me back down the block, and I saw that the sun was up, but it was still so early that no one was outside. We arrived to the playground, where I found my pocketbook, its contents still all over the yard. I was grateful for that. I retrieved my things and thanked them for walking me to my truck. Just then, I noticed that my truck looked low. He had flattened three of my tires. I burst into tears. "What am I going to do now?"

"Don't worry, calm down," Chrishonda said.

We walked back to her grandmother's apartment for a second time—my third. I had to call someone to help me get out of this situation. I didn't want my family to know, but at this point I needed to be rescued more than I needed to save face with them. I called my brother; no answer. I left a message. I then called Leah; she was home. I explained everything to her, and we came up with a plan. She would wire me some money. I had twelve dollars in my coat that I must have put in there from change I had received. I would get a hack to the check-cashing place, and when it opened at eight, I would get the money that Leah was sending and take a cab to the Newark airport. I would then take another cab from the airport to my house. I would get my truck later. That was the best news I had heard all night. I was happy that someone knew what was going on with me. Leah couldn't believe it, and said she was going to phone Bryan. I wasn't concerned with informing anyone; I just wanted to get home.

There was a loud knock on the door. Chrishonda boyfriend went to answer it, and I told Leah it was D. He had found me. I started to cry, and Leah started to cry with me. I explained to her that his cousin had said she wouldn't put me out. Her man came back in, telling me he wanted to speak with me. I told him I was not talking to him. I didn't have anything to say to him. Then the knocking started again. This time, Chrishonda went to the door. When she came back, I knew that I had to leave with him. She looked at me, apologetic. "He said he wouldn't hurt you; he swore on his kids that he wouldn't hurt you," she explained.

"Did you not see what he just did to me and my truck? Please don't do this!" I begged her.

On the phone, Leah was hollering at me not to go with him. She was crying just as hard as I was. She went back to the door. I looked down the hall, where I could see Dashad talking to Chrishonda. He was on his knees, kissing his hands to God. I knew that was it; she wasn't going to protect me anymore. I told Leah that I loved her and would call her when I could. I had to go. I hung up, and all the life went out of me. I was numb walking down that hallway. I opened up the door, and he was standing there looking at me. He motioned for me to come out. I thought, *this is it. He was going to kill me.* We walked down the hall to the elevators. He went in first, and then I got on. Still silence: no one said a word. We got off the elevator. Outside, in the car, were two men, his cousin Blake and some other guy I had never seen before. Dashad grabbed my arm once we got to the backseat of the car, where the guy was sitting, and opened his door. "Is this the pretty lady you saw going into this building?"

"Yeah, that's her," he replied.

Dashad gave him a twenty-dollar bill and thanked him. That was to just let me know that he would find me if he needed to; I could never hide from him. Blake looked at me in dislike. He got out of the front seat and got into the back seat. I got into the car. We drove down the block to drop him off. He said good-bye to Dashad and shot me another nasty look once he got out of the car. We drove off.

Dashad kept trying to speak to me, but I ignored him. He assured me that he wasn't going to hurt me anymore. We pulled up to a familiar spot. It was one of the hotels that we had stayed at from time to time. He told me to follow him. He was a little more calmed down. I followed him inside. Once we got into the room, I sat at the desk right by the door. I was so tired. He began to fill the Jacuzzi with water. He took his pants off and rolled a blunt. I just sat there looking at him, thinking, *who the fuck are you?* Then he told me to get undressed and join him. I told him no. He informed me, "I am asking you nicely. I could *make* you get in here with me." I took my clothes off and got in with him. There were mirrors all around the tub. I looked like a complete mess. My eyes were bloodshot red from crying all night, my hair looked crazy from him pulling on it, and I had scratches on my neck from him grabbing me around my throat trying to get me to come with him. I looked horrible. He asked me to come close to him. He looked me in my face and told me that he was very sorry, but he had been mad that I'd wanted to leave him. I told him I didn't want to be a part of killing someone. He also said he was upset because the cops could have killed him. The police in New York were not like police in other states, he said. He told me he had a friend who was killed by New York cops.

He went on to tell me that he just wanted me to be with him. He knew he had made a mistake; he really was sorry. *Wow*, I thought, *another apology from Dashad*. Maybe he was sorry, but I didn't care. I was going to do what I had to do get back home, and that was it. He gave me a bath and kissed the scratches on my neck. Then we got out of the Jacuzzi. He wanted me to make love to him. I did. Then he went to sleep. I lay awake. I was scared to fall asleep next to him. I didn't trust him.

Room service knocked on the door. I spoke to her through the door, telling her we were OK and didn't need anything. Then I went into the bathroom to try and fix myself up. I heard him moving around in the room, and when I came out, he was getting dressed. He let me know it was time to go.

We went back to his aunt's house. We pulled around back, and I didn't see my truck. I asked him what he had done with it. He told me not to worry, that it must have been towed because it didn't have a sticker on it. He would get it later. I didn't want to go to his aunt's house because of all that had happened last night, but he didn't care. We walked in, and everyone was just staring at us. I went straight to the bathroom; I looked a hot mess. He went to lie down in his cousin's room.

His Aunt came into the bathroom to talk with me. She was worried about me and was wondering if I was OK. I needed her cell to let Leah know I was all right and to see if she had sent the money. I informed her about my plan for getting home. I needed someone to take me to get the money from the check-cashing place, being that my car had been impounded. I asked Dashad's aunt to tell him that she needed me to take her someplace. He was tired, so he would have asked me to take her anyway. I told her I would give her fifty dollars. She agreed. She told him she needed to go to the market for some things for dinner. He agreed, but said not to take too long. Once we left the building, she said to me that she didn't think leaving was a good idea. I asked why. "What if he beats you back at your house, what will you do then?" My mouth just dropped. "It would make him like the incredible hulk if he knew you left him," she continued. I understood what she was saying. I realized that I couldn't win, and that there was no way out of this situation—or out of this relationship. I just said a little prayer that God would protect me.

We got back just in time; he was just getting up. We were going to find out where my truck was so we could go home. He called the police to see where it would have been taken, but there was no record of my truck being towed. "Oh my God, someone stole my truck!" I shouted.

"Calm down, I will handle this," he said.

"Who steals a car with three flat tires?" I yelled.

I was floored: in one twenty-four hour period, I been hit on the head with a bottle, choked, had my clothes ripped off of me, been chased down the street, had my tires slashed, and been hunted down by a madman. And now my truck had been stolen. What else could happen?

I phoned my mother, letting her know what had happened—which is good, because when I talked to her, she would have picked up from my demeanor that something was wrong. Dashad got on the phone with her and assured her that he would take care of it. She was relaxed after she spoke to him. He had a way of doing that with people. She told me not to worry about anything; she would take care of everything on her end. She told me she loved me, I told her I loved her, too, and we hung up. I knew my mom would make sure everything was right down there, which put my mind at ease. I know she would plan a fun-filled night in minutes. The children would only miss me a little.

At this point I was really numb. He just kept telling me not to worry about my truck: they would find it. We drove home, and I slept the whole ride. I didn't want to talk to him. We arrived at my house. I had never been so glad to be back home. I got out and slammed the door. He followed me into the house.

"No see you later?" he asked. That was what I always said before we left each other.

"See you later." I went upstairs and locked my door. I needed to be alone. I started some bath water. I heard him drive off and I called my mom and Leah to let them know I was home safe. After I got off the phone, I looked toward the ceiling and said "Thanks." I took a deep breath and got in the tub. I was very grateful to be home.

Chapter Seven

Lost

Luckily it was cool enough outside that I could get away with wearing turtlenecks. I wore them until the scratches healed. Neosporin and Mederma helped a great deal.

I spoke with Leah and asked her not to let anyone know about what had happened. She told me she had already spoken to Bryan. I had figured that much; I'd meant anyone else. She understood, but she wanted this to never happen again. She wanted me to leave him. I couldn't; I was afraid, and I loved him.

I didn't see Dashad for a week. I was intentionally busy when he called. He didn't push; he knew this time he was wrong. So he gave me some time. He called me and said that the police had found my truck. I would have to ride with him to go get it.

He came and picked me up. We hardly said anything on the way up there. He did let me know that Bryan had spoken to him about the incident. Leah had told him everything. Bryan had let Leah onto some things that were helpful. Dashad and his baby mother, Stephanie, fought like that all the time. That was kind of normal for them. That was crazy, I thought. *How can any man putting his hands on you be normal?* Maybe she was afraid, like I was. Who knew?

As we got closer to the impound where my truck was, he started saying nasty things to me. I guess he knew that I wanted to leave him. He told me that I didn't have any friends and that no one was going to want me, with three children. I turned to him and said, "You did. Why wouldn't another man want me?" He informed me that I was ruined for another man. They weren't like him. They wouldn't appreciate me like he did, they wouldn't ignore my flaws like he did, they wouldn't appreciate how deep I was, and they would only want pussy. I let him know that yes, 90 percent of him was wonderful. But the other 10 percent, he was the incredible hulk. Who wanted to deal with that? Not to mention his other life. I reminded him that I put up with his flaws, too. I told him I didn't care what he was saying: "I am a great woman, and there is a man out there that will appreciate me—like you said you did."

He paid the man at the lot, and I got in my truck and drove off.

I cried most of the way. I turned on the radio, and Heather Headley's "I Wish" was playing. That made me cry harder. He followed me onto the highway, but I wasn't aware of it until he pulled up to the side of my truck. He saw that I was crying. He motioned me to pull over at the rest stop before my exit.

I pulled over, and he got out of his car and came to the driver's side window. "What's wrong with you?" he asked. I couldn't believe it, even though I could tell he was sincere. He didn't want me to be upset. He asked again.

"What do you mean all of this? Why are you doing this to me?" I asked.

He stared at me for a second, then walked around the front of the truck and came to the passenger door. He motioned for me to open up the door. I unlocked the door and he got in.

"I am apologizing."

"Are you?"

"Yes. Those things I said were hurtful and not true. You would make any man a great wife. I was mad, so I said those things to hurt you. I thought you were leaving me." He went on about how when people know they are about to get fired, they don't come to work on time or do their job 100 percent. That was the case here, he said. He thought I was going to fire him. I should have. But he didn't want me to leave, he wanted me to stay. He didn't want me to be with anyone else. I made him happy. He said things were going to change. I should just keep believing in him, and things would get better. Was I crazy? I took him back again.

Over the next couple of months, things didn't get better. I noticed a change in myself. I was losing weight. I wasn't completely happy. I was just existing in the world. I didn't have any energy to do anything. I just wanted to lie around. I was depressed.

The treatment started getting worse; the way he talked to me was different than the way he normally spoke to me. Every time I would call him, he would have to call me back, and it would take him a day or two to get back to me. The lovemaking was even different. The funny thing is that I was losing him, but he wanted to be with me. He became more possessive, wanted me in the house all the time. I was confused. I felt like I was his property, not his woman. He would demand instead of ask. There was force where he should be gentle. This was very unclear to me, and it messed with me mentally. I felt withdrawn from the world, like no light was shining on me at all. Everything seemed very grim.

My mom and Leah came over to spend some time with me; I guess it was some kind of intervention. They brought my favorite chocolate to make me feel better, Hershey's with almonds. It only made me think of Dashad; it was one of the things we both enjoyed. That was sweet of them, letting me know I was stronger than I thought and that I could pull myself out of this slump that I was in. "Think of the children and everyone that loves you," they told me. They were right: I had to get out of this. He was only a man. I had to get my strength back. I started going to the gym three days out of the week. I started forcing myself to eat so that I would have the energy that I needed to be a great mom, the mom that I was.

Dashad started to fuss about me going to the gym, and even the market. He told me that most grocery stores deliver to your house. He wanted me home, where no one was looking at me or talking to me. He would come in and asked me who had smiled at me that day. Who thinks of these things? I had learned not to say anything: who knew what kind of mood he might be in? All he did was complain, all the time now. I went from being perfect to not being able to get a thing right, and he had no problem letting me know he wasn't happy. I was a caged animal, a dying flower. I pushed harder to make him happy, taking more from myself. He would summon me in the middle of the night to come to his bed. I would rush to him, only to be a piece of meat that he wanted to jump on. That became regular: no talking unless he wanted to have sex.

We argued sometimes. I couldn't hold it in all the time. I would tell him I wasn't a doll that he could put on the shelf when he was done playing with me. He explained to me that I was his and he could do with me as he wished.

He asked me, "If I gave my dog Blu an expensive T-bone steak, would he have to eat it when I gave it to him?" I looked at him puzzled. He looked back, waiting for an answer. I said no. He went on, "It's his choice, because once I gave it to him, it was his to do with what he pleases. He could eat it then, or he could dig a hole and eat it a week later. It doesn't matter." I was speechless.

I was losing myself. What had happened to the strong, independent woman who knew where she was going? All that was wrapped up in a man—one who paid the bills and provided so well for my family. The weight loss was so visible that he even started to complain. If I lost another pound, he told me, he was going to leave me alone. I guess that was motivation for me to get it together. He was the reason I was not myself. I was afraid that if I did anything wrong, he would hit me. I was worried that I would lose him and all of this would be for nothing. I felt like I was addicted: I had to have me some Dashad. What if he was right—*would* anyone else love me like he said he did? Would they love my children, respect my family? So many questions and no answers. I got myself together, trying to become the woman that he first saw that day in the apartment. I had to get my mind and body right. I got my weight back up, started feeling good about myself. Things were good. We were going back out, having dinner, and going to shows. He started spending time with me and the kids again. He even talked to me in a pleasing tone. I couldn't believe it, but things were starting to turn around.

Chapter Eight

Her

My cells rings and I answer it,
"Hello?"
"Who is this?" the voice questioned.
"Hello?" I asked again.
"You whore, stay away from my man. He has a family."
I could hear a familiar voice in the background, telling her to hang up. I just hung up the phone. I knew it was her; she must have gone through Dashad's phone. My cell rang back a couple of times, saying private. I ignored it. That wasn't for me to deal with. Things were going so well with Dashad. I guess you can't have two households and keep both of them happy at the same time.

Maybe I was wrong, but if he didn't care, why should I? He came to me because he wanted to be here: we shared no kids, no home, none of that. He was with me because he wanted to be here, not for any other reason. I understood that he loved his daughter, and like he said, that had nothing to do with me.

I hadn't been affected until now. She called my phone all night and left crazy but funny messages. She told me I was a whore, a slut, a bitch. I must be desperate; I couldn't get my own man. She was going to kick my ass if she ever saw me. My thoughts were: *this girl is funny*. I was his friend—and those other things, when he asked me—and if she were on the job like she was supposed to be, he wouldn't come looking for me. I was far from desperate, and I did have my own man: Dashad. *Don't let the brownie baking, sports mom shit fool you, I can bring it when need be*, I thought. I saw that this bitch might be a problem. I had to turn it off. Dashad called the house phone, apologizing for the situation. He said he had fallen asleep waiting for her to get his daughter ready, and she had gone through his phone. I was the last person he had called.

We spoke of what had happened for a second. I told him what she had said, and he told me to change my number. I explained that I couldn't do that, because was my business number also. He insisted and said he would pay for it. When we got off the phone, I called the company to change the number immediately. They did. I called my mom and the store to give them the new number. My brother was at work; he asked if I was OK, and told me that if I ever need to talk, he was there. I wasn't fooling anyone; everyone could tell that something was going on. I told him I would come to him if I needed. "I'm OK," I told him, "I just keep getting prank calls."

The next day Dashad called me on the house phone and asked me for the new number to my cell. I gave it to him. He also wanted my password. I asked why, and he said because he wanted it. I saw now how we got into it. Everything that he went through, I went through. I *was* affected by his other life. When Stephanie got on his nerves, he was with me—and vice versa. Those couple of months when I was going through it, everything was good over there. Now that it was good with us, there was trouble over there. I realized that a man couldn't make two women happy. Someone always missed out. But like everything else, it was swept under the rug. He would make me feel like I was the only woman for him: that was why I didn't worry about her.

Months went by without a problem. We took our weekly trip to New York, and this time we brought Amir and Nya; Amirah had a slumber party to go to, so she stayed with my mom. The family loved my children, they commented on how cute and well-mannered they were. Amir fit right in with his younger cousins. As usual, the men and women separated. It had been about six months since I had been to see anyone outside my immediate family, ever since that mess happened with D. No one judged me for it; they knew he loved me, and I loved him. Anyway they went through stuff like that with their own men. It seemed to be common to have a fight with you baby daddy or your boo—as they called their boyfriends. The children played well with Anya. Dashad had a lot of cousins, and a lot of them had babies, so it was like Nya was in play land. There were so many little friends for her to play with. My son was also ecstatic that he had so many new cousins to play with and come back and visit. I come from a small family, with one or two cousins per household. I loved being around all the kids, and so did my children. We'd had a great time, but we had to get back on the highway. Being that we had the kids, we couldn't stay long. Before too long, we were home.

I went to get Nya ready for bed, and my men decided to play basketball outside. While we were in New York, Amir was playing basketball with Dashad's younger cousins, and D saw that he had potential. Basketball was his game. They played for me. Amir won. I am fairly sure Dashad let him win, but maybe not.

Dashad stayed the night, and I got up early to make French toast. I needed to go out and get some eggs and cinnamon. Dashad's car was in back of my truck, I didn't wake him; I just took his car to the market. I was racing down the aisles getting some of the things I needed in the house since I was at the store, but I knew I had to hurry back before any of the kids woke up. They would have a heart attack. I jumped in the car, not paying attention to my surroundings, and made a right on a no right turn.

The officer was right there, and he couldn't ignore that. He put his lights on like I knew he was going to. I pulled over. I reached for the glove box and opened it to get the proof of registration and insurance out, and noticed a used pregnancy test in there. I gave the officer all my paperwork, but my focus was on the stick. I told him I was sorry; I was rushing home and hadn't seen the sign. He told me to hold on. He went back to his patrol car and got in. I reached over to get the stick out and read it. It was faded. I haven't taken a test in a minute, so I didn't know what it meant. What if that bitch was pregnant? Oh my God, what was happening? I put it back and decided I would have to do some research on this. The officer came back to the car and gave me my paperwork. He informed me I had a clean driving record and told me to try to keep it that way. I thanked him and drove off. When I got back, everyone was still sleep. I took the opportunity to call the pharmacy and ask the clerk to interpret the test. She wasn't sure; I would have to know what kind of test it was from. The only way I could find out was by calling his cousin. But I had seen her yesterday, and she had said nothing.

I called her and left message for her to call me. I went on like nothing happened. I didn't want to start something and ruin everything, but he had made it seem like to me he was just there for his child. Of course he loved her, he was honest about that but, he was still fucking her with no condom. Putting me at risk. I said nothing. I needed more to bring up the subject. I prepared breakfast and went about as normal.

Later that week, we took a trip back to see his family. It was someone's birthday. I saw Latisha and asked her why she hadn't called me back. She told me that Dashawn had put her phone in the toilet. She couldn't get it to work; it had to dry out. I pulled her to the side and asked her about Stephanie—was she pregnant? She just looked at me and stared. My heart dropped.

"She is, isn't she?" I asked.
"She called me yesterday and told me," she explained.
"Has he told you yet?" I asked.
"No. Not a word. How did you find out?" she asked.
I told her that I had found a test in his glove compartment.
I just stood there, lifeless. Why would he do that to me? How could he hide this? I felt really bad, like I had the flu. I looked like it, too, according to Latisha. I just looked across the street at him in disgust. He was laughing and joking with his cousins on the block. She told me not to worry; Stephanie might not have it. But I thought she might; she needed something to hold onto to him. A baby would do just that. He was a great father. Just because he didn't want it didn't mean this time she would get rid of it. I told Latisha I was going to go sit in the car. She apologized. I told her it wasn't her fault. I went across the street and got into the car. I opened up the glove box, and the test was still in there. I don't think he knew it was. That was for me to find it. Why would he leave it in there? Latisha came over and asked me to walk her to the store. I really didn't feel like it, so I told her I would watch the baby for her. He got in and grabbed the steering wheel and started acting like he was driving. Dashad came over and asked why I didn't want to walk to the store. I looked up at him and almost cried. He asked what was wrong. I told him I wasn't feeling well. He asked if I was hungry, and I told him no. He let me know that we were about to go get something to eat; what did I want? I just put my head down. He got in the backseat and asked me repeatedly what was wrong. I explained that nothing was, I just didn't feel good. He knew that I knew, and he also knew that his cousin had confirmed it. He took Dashawn out of the car and gave him to one of his cousins, and then he told them we had to leave. I was a little nervous; I didn't want him to start with me. I didn't have the energy. He told me we were meeting a couple of his cousin's downtown to eat. We had some time to kill, so did I want to go get my hair done? It didn't matter what I wanted; we went anyway. I sat in the lady's chair, and she gave me some books to pick what I wanted. I chose something simple, a flat twist into a bun: we didn't have a lot of time. He told her to do whatever I wanted. I still sat there, with little life in me. I was about to

lose a big part of my life. He sat there the whole time except to take a phone call, looking at me. The stylist was finally done. She showed me in the mirror, and it did look pretty, very pretty, but I didn't feel pretty. I felt like shit. The ladies started talking in French, like they always do and Dashad went to pay. I went to the bathroom before we left. He told me they were talking about me, saying I was ungrateful and didn't deserve him, that he was trying to be nice and I had my face all poked out. I guess his knowing many languages did come in handy sometimes. He knew something was wrong with me, and even they had noticed. I continued to deny that anything was wrong.

We headed downtown to meet his family. He asked me to cheer up. I did, a little; I didn't want to spoil the night. His phone rang, and someone on the other end gave him directions. He hung up, and we parked. We got out and walked. He was holding me so close to him. I loved the way he smelled. He kissed me and said I looked beautiful. I smiled. It's true: if you smile, it can change your mood. We stopped in front of a pair of gold doors. He went in first, holding the door for me. We walked into a foyer with red walls and a Japanese print. Then we went through two more big doors. I would have never expected the scene in front of me. It was so beautiful. I lost my train of thought. People were laughing, smiling, and dining in their best, and there were waiters all around, looking like penguins assisting everyone with their needs, very attentive. The lighting was perfect, and the huge floral arrangement of tulips filled the room with a pleasant smell. I couldn't believe all the diamond jewelry that I saw, just sparkling. Necklaces, watches and earrings.

I excused myself to the restroom. I was so uncomfortable. I had on blue jeans, a white shirt, a jean jacket and white K-Swiss sneakers. I was clearly underdressed. I asked a lady in the restroom, who had on a nice black dinner dress, what kind of restaurant this was, and she said Mr. Chow's. "You have never been here before?" she asked. I said no. She continued to say that people came there for anniversaries, birthdays, and special occasions. She asked why I was there, what was I celebrating? I told her, "He just asked me if I was hungry." She smiled and said he was a good guy to bring me there. She told me to enjoy, and I told her the same. As I went to wash my hands, I thought, *my hair done and now this, he knows that I know but I don't care.* The restaurant was beautiful. He was really saying sorry, and I forgave him. We would deal with this issue later, but right now we would enjoy our night together.

I came back out with a whole new attitude. He could tell, and he was very happy that I was.

"Would you like a drink?" he asked. "The table won't be ready for a minute."

"No thank you, I can wait. This is very nice, thank you."

"You're welcome," he said smiling.

He knew he had me. I was like a little child observing everything that was going on and trying to pick up little pointers to make my restaurant more productive. His cousins finally joined us. They seemed excited to be dinning there, too. The hostess walked us to our table. It was a nice, cozy table in the corner, private. We sat down, and then a waiter appeared.

"Welcome to Mr. Chow's. How may I help you?"

"We weren't given menus yet." Dashad informed him.

"I am the menu." All of us looked up at him. That was something new, no menu. OK. "What do you feel like tonight, beef, seafood, chicken . . . ?"

He looked at me first, as I was the only lady present. I knew what I wanted, anyway.

"I would like seafood," I said

"Seafood for the lady. And for the gentlemen?"

They chose chicken and beef; Dashad chose chicken to be on the safe side. The waiter suggested that we try the appetizers, and Dashad agreed, told him to bring them all out, and we would try them all.

"Very well," he said, and then he left the table.

It was wonderful. I forgot all about what was going on. It was like we had just met again. After we left the restaurant, we walked a couple of blocks, just walking and talking about the evening and different things. He was going to sell his house. I didn't ask why, just listened. He stopped to buy me a bouquet of roses from a flower shop. The evening was perfect. How could I let this man go? Where would I get another Dashad?

Weeks went by, and I had a new sense of self. My life was back to normal: the restaurant and my children and Dashad.

I got a phone call from her off of Dashad's phone—the same stuff: you ho, you bitch. She kept asking me who I was. The thing that puzzled me is that she thought I was a different woman. She went on to tell me that he had a girlfriend and a family. I asked her why she was calling me.

I didn't know who she was. I told her to please stop calling my phone. She never said Dashad's name. She let me know that my number had showed up on her man's phone many times, and that she knew exactly how long we had talked on the phone. Was she serious? *I* didn't even know how long we had talked. All of a sudden, the phone hung up. I guess he found out that she was on his phone.

This time I was upset. I was tired of her calling me with the mess, and upset with him for being so sloppy. Why did he set his phone down if he knew she was going to go through it? Leave it in the car or something. I was tired of this.

He called me right back, and I could tell he was riled up. He apologized, but I wasn't trying to hear it this time. He told me I had to change my number again. I refused. "I am not doing back flips for this bitch. I don't care what you have to do; I am not changing my number. Stop laying your phone down, erase my number, or something. I am not doing it," I said.

"There's no need to call her names," he said.

"Oh, but she can call me all kinds of names."

"You should be the bigger person," he said. I just hung up. I didn't have time for this. I wanted to be left alone. He called me back. I didn't answer, and then I turned off my phone.

The next morning, I called him. Amirah had a question for him: why were Cuban cigars illegal in the United States? I called and got no answer. I continued to get the kids ready, and my cell rang back. It was Dashad.

"Hey," I said.

"Who the fuck is this? Look, bitch, I told you he has a woman!" I just lost it.

"First of all, I am nobody's bitch, so stop calling me that. My name is Isis. I am not a ho, slut, or whatever you want to call me. I am his friend. You are going to stop calling my phone with this bullshit. I called Dashad's phone, not your phone. A number that was giving to me by Dashad. I don't know what your problem is, but I will call him when I get damn ready and you're not going to stop me! I have entertained this shit for a minute. It is actually childish. You keep your problems inside your house. You have an issue with him, you address him. Stop calling my fucking phone." Then I hung up. My daughter came to ask if I was all right. I told her yes and that we would get the answer online. Then my phone rang again. I ignored it and then turned it off. I got the kids off to school and went back home to relax. I called Leah. I hadn't been talking to anyone about our problems, but I didn't know what to do.

"Damn, why haven't you told me all of this before?" Leah asked, sighing. That was a lot for her to take in. I had to tell her everything. She continued. "You have to leave that niggah alone. Fuck that, him putting his hands on you, he don't own your ass!"

I explained to her that I just was hoping that it would get better. I did believe in him. Yeah, maybe I was stupid for taking him back, but I just wanted to forgive him. I loved him, why wouldn't I forgive him? It was very complicated, the way I saw it, but she didn't care. She wanted me out. She had a remedy, too: if he was to come back after I left him, she knows some dudes that would break his legs. I imagined she was talking about some Italians. I explained that it didn't need to go that far.

My phone had beeped. It was Dashad; I told Leah I would call her back.

"Hello?" I said, not happy.

"Why would you tell her that?" He sounded so pissed.

"Oh no, you are not going to change this and make this about me."

"I told you—just hang up."

"I'm sick of her calling me all kinds of fucking names."

"Are you a bitch?"

I didn't answer. He repeated himself. "Well, are you?"

"No," I said with shame. Just like that, he'd made me feel bad about what had happened, when it wasn't my fault. I wasn't being childish, that bitch was being ghetto.

"Do you want to be the one that comes in between me and my kids?" he shouted.

Me being me, I read between the lines. "Kids? What do you mean by *kids*, what happened to *daughter*?" That was the perfect way to open it up. I had been waiting for months to see what had been up with this. There was a moment of silence. I just hung up.

I had a headache in the back of my eyeball. It was intense. I picked up the phone and called Leah back. I informed her had just happened. I was shocked: I didn't get a crazy response from her. She just told me to leave him alone: "I told you he was no good." I think she knew. She and Bryan shared a lot. If the shoe had been on the other foot, I would have been devastated, but she wasn't. She'd had time to digest the information. That was it, I was officially insane. I hung up with Leah. I paced the floor, and then I lay on the couch and cried, holding one of the pillows. I had so many thoughts going through my head. That was it: I was done with Dashad. All this shit plus another baby? Oh, hell no.

I turned my phone back on after awhile. I had messages, but I just deleted them. It could have been business. I didn't care. That was another problem: this was affecting my business. I just lay around for hours thinking of what was I going to do.

Later that night, I called Dashad. He answered. You could tell he really didn't want to talk about it; he was still mad at me. I wanted us to talk about it, for him to understand my side. He was too preoccupied with making things right with her. I asked him what he was thinking about, and he told me the only thing he was worrying about was how to get back into his house. I didn't ask him again, I just repeated it back in my head: *he said he was only worrying about getting back into his house.* Yeah, I'd heard him right. I told him calmly that I would talk to him later. That surprised him, but he didn't really give it any thought after that. I hung up. I stood there for a second, repeated it again in my head, and then started walking through the house grabbing Dashad's things. I went to my room first. I grabbed the overnight bag with all the ho pumps, sexy lingerie, makeup, and toys that he liked. I went through the drawers and got all of his clothes out of the them. I took the Ali and Sonny Liston picture that I had brought him for a birthday present one year down from my wall. I got together all the cards, gifts, and bears he had bought over the years, all the poems I had written to him. I went to the bathroom and got his robe, his toothbrush, and his slippers. I got ashtrays, cigars, Goya cans, any Spanish seasoning that was in the cabinet. I walked through the house collecting little things. Amirah asked me what I was doing. She could see that I wasn't myself and that I was going from room to room grabbing all of Dashad's things. I assured her I was fine, had never seen more clearly. I knew I was crazy for this one, but I gave back the six hundred dollars he had given me earlier that week. Yes, I gave it all back. I stuck the bags in the back of my truck and hopped in and drove off.

Now, during the course of our relationship, Dashad had told me some things about his kid's mother, about their situation. The house that they live in is in his name. He had bought that before they got together. One day I had gotten into D's car, riding with him to New York and in the back seat was some mail. It was her Verizon bill; either he was going to pay it, or she had left it in the car. My guess was that he didn't know it was there, that she had left it. If he had known that was in the backseat, he would have hidden it, like other things he had hidden from me. We stopped on the turnpike so he could use the restroom. I stayed in the car. Once he was out of sight, I got the mail off of the seat. It was addressed to Stephanie Butts. I goggled the address, and since then I have always known where the house was. I never needed to go there, I gave him that much respect, but now I could have cared less.

I arrived at the house. D's car wasn't there. I started taking out his things, gathering them up and putting them on the front stoop. I brought the last bag onto the step, and then I knocked on the door. I knocked again, but no one answered. I walked away from the door, heading back down the walkway to my truck. I wasn't satisfied; it felt like someone was in there. I turned around. I went back and knocked on the door, and someone spoke from inside.

"Who is it?" they asked.

"Is D here?" I asked.

"Who?" they asked again.

I was tired of playing this game. "Is Dashad there?" I asked. That would let whoever was on the opposite side of that door known that I knew him. I knew his real name.

All of a sudden, the door opened. It was her. She was big pregnant; her stomach was out there. I just kept looking at her: she was not cute at all. She questioned me some more: "Who are you? Are you Isis?"

"Yes, I'm Isis."

"You were with girl on the phone the other night?"

I ignored her question and asked her, "Is Dashad here?" She said,

"No!" and lunged at me, grabbing the top of my jacket. She had a good grip, too. I slung her around and to the ground, to get her off of me.

"Let go of me!" I said calmly. "I came here, I ain't scared of you." Everybody wants to be a bully. No one really wants to fight, just my thoughts anyway. To win, you must take your opponent's power from them; my granny told me that. She was supposed to be some kind of badass. Stephanie stood up, and I just kept looking at her belly. She asked me "Why did you come to my house?" with a nasty tone. I turned to her and said, "This is his house." Right there, she knew that we were involved and deep. Dashad is a private person, and for me to know these private things, she knew I wasn't just some ho, bitch or slut.

"Look! I came here to drop off his things. I'm done with him."

"No, I want you to stay. I'm calling him now." She dialed and didn't get an answer. She tried again. His lying cheating ass was probably with someone else; he'd told me all he wanted to do was get back in his house. His house was calling, and he wasn't answering.

"Come in," Stephanie said.

"I am not coming in that house so he can be trying to beat my ass!"

"*He hits you? Oh my God!*" she acted like she was mad that I said that. What kind of sick mess was this? She was walking in circles, talking to herself. She couldn't believe it. I just turned around and walked away. I didn't look back, either.

I was almost home when Dashad called my cell. "What the fuck do you want?" I asked.

"You came to my house?"

"Sure did. Go ahead, front for her." In the background I could hear her asking, "Where does she live at, Dashad?"

"Don't you ever come anywhere near my family again," he warned me.

"Fuck you!" I hung up.

Ten minutes later, he called me back. I answered the phone. He said, "Thank you, now I don't have to hide anymore."

I got back to my house. Everyone was asleep. That was a good thing. I was upset, and I didn't want anyone to see me mad. I called Leah, and she was on the phone with Mo. I guess Bryan had called her, and she didn't know what to do, so she had called Monique. They called me right back.

"Is you crazy?" Leah asked.

"Fuck him! I hate him!"

"Calm down. What happened? Why did you go there?" asked Monique.

"He told me the only thing he was worried about was getting back in the house with her. I'm tired of him talking to me like I'm not shit. Fuck him!"

"You know what? That's what he gets. This shit had to come to an end sometime," said Leah.

"This is him now. He called me earlier and told me thank you."

"Thank you for what?" asked Mo.

"He doesn't have to hide no more. He can confess to it all. She gonna forgive him, and he'll be back. Things will be back to normal," Leah explained.

"What—you took demented in college?" asked Mo.
"Why does he keep calling?" I asked.
"That isn't him, it's her." said Monique.
I clicked over, "What do you want?"
"Where do you live at? I'm coming to see you," she screamed.
"Ask Dashad." And I hung up.
"They're coming over here. Now she wants to be tough. I was just there, and she was trying to ask me questions."
"They aren't coming over there," said Leah.
Monique asked, "How do you know? Call the police!"
"He ain't bringing her over there because he can never go back to Isis's house again. This is not the first time he has got busted. He know he gonna have to play it close for a couple weeks, but he ain't leaving you alone," Leah informed us.
"How the hell do you know all of this?" I asked.
"He ain't any different from any other man."
"I can't believe this." I broke down crying.
"It's gonna be alright," insisted Monique.
"Girl, don't worry about him. You're better off," Leah said.

My phone kept beeping, but they told me not to answer it. I wanted to; I wanted to get some things off of my chest. They were right, though. No one was hearing anything anyone said it: was just a whole lot of shouting. I was broken inside—how could he talk to me like that? I told the girls thank you and that I would talk with them later. They both told me to call them anytime if I needed to talk. I was glad that I had my girls; they had my back. Friends are hard to come by. I just wanted to go to sleep. My phone rang in the middle of the night. It was Dashad. The first time I ignored it, but he called again, I answered, but didn't say anything.

"So you're done with me?" He asked.

I didn't answer him. "She's never going to leave me now," he said. Then he hung up.

Why was he doing this to me, what did he mean? He wanted to be with her. The mental games just continued.

I called Leah back and told her what he had said. She told me again that she knew he wasn't going to leave me alone. He had made a mistake by saying he was only worried about her; he was mad at me, but that wasn't any reason for him to leave me. Men leave woman for cheating, or stealing, not for this. He understood that all that shit was getting on my nerves. He knew he should have had more control over her actions. "Any woman would have done what you did," Leah told me. "Don't be worried about what he thinks. The hell with him; that's what he gets. He's playing games with you, trying to make you feel bad."

She must have taken some kind of course. How did she know all that about the male psyche?

"How do you know all that?" I asked

"Life. You let him get away with a lot of things. I am not saying it was bad on your part, but you did let him get away with a lot. So he just kept doing what he wanted. He ain't going anywhere. Trust me. He has to make things right with her. Watch. He'll be back."

Chapter Nine

Who Am I?

I didn't talk to Dashad for three weeks. Not one call, not one text, nothing. I felt like I was losing my mind the first week, then the second week it was easier. I was starting to get over the whole mess. I told the children that he'd gone to Seattle, Washington to open another barber shop. I told my mom and brothers the same lie. I didn't want to be looked at as the woman with three failed relationships. I know it wasn't me. It was the men that chose me. That was where I went wrong; I should have chosen them instead.

Then, one day when I went to work like normal, I pulled up and Dashad was in front of the restaurant waiting. No one else was around. I got out of the truck, and he got out of his car. I looked over at him, and then proceeded to the door. He walked toward the front of the door. I stopped and asked him what he wanted. He let me know that he was there to talk to me. Everything must have been in the clear; he made everything right with her, just like Leah said. I hated that I was out of the loop with certain things about relationships. But what I didn't know, Leah would tell me. I asked him to talk about what was going on with his family. He said he was sorry, but what was he supposed to do? He loved his children, and he wasn't going to be apart from them. He reminded me that he already had two other children, and their mom was married to someone else. "I promised myself that I would be there this time—I'm not going to lose that," he told me. "It's cool," I informed him. "You don't have to lose them. You lost me." He told me that I would always be his. I just stood at the door. He wanted to go in. At first I refused, but Aurora had given me a night stick, in case I ever had a problem again. I let him in, but positioned my bag so that if he did try something, I would be ready. He looked down at my bag. He must have known. I could never play poker; I would give my hand away. Anyway, we sat down. He let me know that he was very upset with me and sorry at the same time. He was sorry about what he had said to me, and told me that if he could take it back, he would. He couldn't see me without him, with another. "I never thought you would tell on me," he said. "Diary" was our song, and he sang some of the chorus: "I won't tell your secrets, just think of me as a page in your Diary—I trusted you." He was unbelievable, so selfish. All he thought of was himself. "You would rather hurt yourself and the ones you love to have what you don't deserve. I trusted you, too, and lost all across the board," I told him. "Why are you here? What do you need?"

"You. I want you to come with me."

"What? I am not going *anywhere* with you!"

"I need you."

"I'm not going with you anywhere!"

"What, you don't trust me?"

"*No*! I don't."

"If I wanted to jump on you, nothing would stop me. I want to talk to you."

"Is that what you normally do? I have work to do."

I started to walk through the back, turning the lights and the ovens on, bringing in the bread. He followed and helped with the bread.

"I need to talk to you."

"Then talk!" I insisted.

"Privately."

I just looked at him.

"I miss you," he went on. "I'm sorry, and I want to make it up to you."

"How many times can I forgive you?"

"As many as it takes to get it right. You said you loved me."

I explained to him that there wasn't anyone to cover me. I had to stay at the restaurant. He informed me that he was going to get a room because he was tired. I was shocked that he didn't ask to go to the house. Or maybe he was already there, and knew that I had changed the locks. He told me he would call me, and when I got a minute I should come to the room. He let me know how he missed me. The way he said it, I know he meant sexually. I loved him, and I did want to make it work. How could I have let things get so far gone? He still had a hold on me.

I started my day, and when my brother came in, I let him know I had some errands to do. I went and met Dashad.

Once I got there, we talked about what had happened. He said the way I reacted was like he had shot my mother. I explained to him that I had lost it, but I had given him everything. For him to tell me that he was only worried about someone else was just too much: he could have her and leave me alone. That was my attitude that day. He asked if I still felt that way. He also asked how I had felt when she opened up the door and I saw her pregnant. I told him it made me even more outraged. I didn't want to relive that, I told him.

He told me that all they did was fight that night. She hit him in the head with one of the Goya cans I put with his stuff. She knew that I wasn't just some bitch he was sleeping with. All the Valentine's gifts, gifts period, the money, all the items that I gave back, they told her that he had a life with me. Even though she knew that, she wasn't letting go. I knew he would never leave her alone, either. They were a family. I would always be the extra.

Even through all of this, he still wanted to be with me. There would be different rules.

I believed he was here because he wanted some ass; she'd had the baby three weeks ago and she was mad at him for cheating. He wanted me all right. He was backed up. I was, too, but I wasn't thinking about sex until he started touching me. We did the deed. I felt bad afterwards. I should have left him alone, but I loved him. This wouldn't get better; it would just get worse. I didn't want to let go, and neither did he. We lay there for hours, him telling me how we could make things better for us. *I am stronger than this*, I thought, but I was in love; nothing could change that.

I continued to see Dashad, secretly. No one was to know, not even Leah. I hated that I had to lie to my friends. He told me he didn't like Leah: she was always in our business. She was my friend—she was *supposed* to look out for me. It was Bryan telling her all his business; Dashad should check him. He told me he wouldn't let anyone know what he was doing anymore either. He couldn't trust anyone. He said he wished he had met me on South Street: none of this would have ever happened. Yeah, I would have been in the dark about a lot of things. I was once told that if you have to do something in the dark, you don't need to do it at all.

That day at the hotel, when I told him that I had to go and get back to the restaurant, he handed me a blank CD. He told me to play it when I got in the truck, and to call him after I listened to it. It was Lyfe Jennings, "Let's Stay Together." I listened to it twice, and then I called him and forgave him. I told him we would have to work through this together.

I was a fool to agree to continue seeing him. I would see him once a week, and every now and then he would call to check up on me. These were two-second conversations. I had gone from greatness to nothing in a matter of three years. It went on like that for about a year. He would get away when he could, and we were happy to see one another.

How had it come to this? Maybe I *was* a desperate woman. I was a coward—I didn't want to start over, or be by myself. Who would love me? Was this even love? Or did I really think in the back of my mind that he would leave her and we would be a family? If I looked in a mirror, I wouldn't know have known myself right then. I had let this man come into my world after all that I had been through and turn it right back around—and not in a good way. This was the pits.

We didn't have a relationship; we didn't share, really. We met; it seemed, only to have sex. He couldn't be away for many hours without her blowing up his phone. I tried to leave, but every time I would he would do something to win me back.

Aurora called me to go out and celebrate; she had been promoted on her job. I had told Dashad the night before that I was done with him, so this was perfect. I could go out and let off some steam. We chose the 40/40 club in Atlantic City. We went shopping before we went to the club. It felt good to get out. I brought sexy some boots from Macy's. She got a couple of things, too, and then we left. I went home to get ready, and so did she. While I was getting ready, Dashad's aunt called me.

"Hello?"

"Hey, girly."

"Hey, Titi! How are you? Is everything OK?"

"Yes, of course, I called to see how you were doing. You've been on my mind lately."

"Oh, how sweet. I'm fine, about to go out with my cousin."

I explained about Aurora's promotion. "We're going to the 40/40 club in Atlantic City." I told Titi that I would call her back. My cousin would be there soon, and I had to finish getting ready. She agreed and told me to be careful. We hung up, and not a second later, my cousin came in hollering for me. It seemed that I was always the last one to get ready. I finished my makeup, and we were out the door. We were both fierce; I knew we were going to have a good time. I left my cell phone home on purpose. No drama.

She knew of some of the mess that I was going through with Dashad. What I loved about my cousin is that she didn't judge either one of us. She knew we loved each other. But tonight was about her. We were going to get it in, and that is what we did. We had an amazing time. We laughed, danced, and had too much to drink. It was nice to be admired by men that didn't even know me. We had a great time, but we had to stop four times on the way home because I was so tired and drunk. She was more out of it than me. Being tired and having liquor in you is a mixture for disaster. I would pull over and sleep for about five or ten minutes, then get back on the highway. We were finally five minutes from my house, but I needed to stop again. I pulled over into a Dunkin' Donuts, the only thing open in the wee hours in the morning. I went into the restroom to splash some water on my face, and when I came out, Aurora had this look on her face. She was motioning to something; I was unclear what until I reached the car. She was trying to tell me that Dashad was on the phone. Oh my God and what the hell—how did he get her number? I grabbed the phone from her.

"What are you doing? What do you want?" I asked in a voice that let him know I was offended.

"Where are you at?" he insisted.

"How did you get her number?"

"I've been calling you all night. I called the house. The nanny finally answered, and I had her wake up Amirah. I told her that I would give her fifty dollars if she would call you on three way for me."

"Baby?"

"Yes, Mom?"

"I am sorry, lay the phone down and go back to bed." I paused for a second to give her time to put down the phone.

"What do you want?" I asked him again.

"Where are you?" he asked.

"Why?"

"I'm in AC."

"So?"

"Where are you at?" he practically screamed.

"I'm almost home."

"What?"

"I'm five minutes from the house."

"Come back down here and get me."

"No, I'm tired."

"I got dropped off down here; I thought you were at the 40/40."

I could kill Titi. I was glad that I had left; she was trying to get me killed. If I had been in there dancing and having a good time when he walked in, he would have dragged me out by my hair in front of everyone.

"I am really tired, and I had a lot to drink."

"Come get me. I paid the bouncer four hundred dollars to let me in that club. I had a T-shirt on, and he wouldn't let me in. I gave him the money that was in my pocket. Come and get me. I'll call you back and tell you were I'm at."

Then he just hung up.

"He's crazy," I told my cousin. "He woke up Amirah so she would call me on three-way. I hate him. He wants me to go back and get him." She said I would be crazy to drive back down there. I let her know that I had to: he had gotten dropped off. I went into the Dunkin' Donuts and bought some coffee. I was going to need it. It was going to be a long drive back down there. We got into the house, and I checked on everyone. Aurora jumped right in my bed. I grabbed my phone; it had thirteen missed calls on it. Ten were from Dashad.

I called him back and asked him where he was. He was at the tables, and he was going to gamble until I got back down there. But he told me to hurry: his phone was dying. I got back on the expressway. I was so tired. I had all the windows open, trying to get some oxygen to my brain. He called me to see if I was on my way. I let him know I was half way there, and then his phone died. All of this was insane. Now his phone was dead. What was I doing on the highway? I needed to be in my bed asleep.

Just then my phone rang with an unfamiliar number. I answered it anyway. He had borrowed someone's phone to call me; he had paid them twenty dollars "to call his wife because his phone died." Wife. Yeah, right. He told me to meet him on the rooftop like we always did. He told me he was winning big, and we were going to stay.

Fifteen minutes later, another call came through. This time it is a lady informing me that the plans had changed. I was to meet him on the boardwalk in front of the Showboat casino. She let me know that he was OK and would be waiting for me.

It was 5:45 in the morning when I arrived in Atlantic City for the second time. I parked the car in our normal spot and started toward the boardwalk. The sun was coming up. I was the only fool on the boardwalk at that time. All of a sudden, my phone rang. It was D.

"Hello?" I answered. "Where are you?"

"Is that you, that fine-ass woman walking in front of the Taj Mahal?"

Just then I saw him, sitting on a bench. He was looking so good, nice shape, face all clean. He had cuffed his jeans with black ACG boots on, looking sexy. I walked up to him. He was just staring at me. "You look very nice, I'm loving the boots." They did look like knee-high hooker boots.

He was so happy to see me. He told me about the nice people who had helped him out with their cell phones when his had died. When he went to cash in his winnings, the cashier let him charge his phone. I am sure he gave her a nice tip.

He grabbed my hand, and we walked onto the sand, towards the water. I didn't understand the direction he was going but I just went with the flow.

He commented about how nice it was, the two of us on the beach and the sun coming up: how romantic was that. He wasn't lying, it was nice. He couldn't have timed it any better. He always made up for whatever dumb thing he did. He was just so original with it, and it wasn't some lame apology; he really wanted to win me back.

I loved the effort he made not to lose me. I wished he would just not do the stupid things that he did. He tried to make love to me right on the beach. I resisted. If we were on some tropical beach that would be just perfect, but we were in Atlantic City, New Jersey. I insisted that he stop.

We went back into the casino. We went from casino to casino looking to get a hotel room. I was so tired I just wanted to sleep. While they were checking, he would go play on the tables for a bit, winning every time. He visited one of the shops while we were waiting and bought me a bottle of Burberry Tender Touch perfume. It smelled delightful.

Finally we got information that Trump Plaza had rooms, and we took a cab over. In the cab, I phoned the nanny and told her I would be staying. She assured me that everyone would be all right. We finally got a room. Dashad told the front desk clerk that we wanted our room "the higher the better."

She gave him the keycard and smiled, telling him it was on the nineteenth floor.

I didn't understand, but I did when we got to the room. It was very nice; the ocean view was so romantic. The room was so tranquil it looked like a presidential suite. I was happy, very happy. I went into the bathroom to wash my face and get out of my clothes. I hadn't slept in twenty-four hours, and my lovely, knee-high boots were killing my feet. When I came out he was enjoying the view, leaning up against the large window that was supported by steel beams. The view was beautiful. It was early morning, the sun was up and the ocean moving, waves crashing on the beach. It was very relaxing.

"This is really nice, thank you," I said.

"I am glad that you came back to get me," he said.

I told him, "let's lie down and take a nap." I should have known that was out of the question. He wanted me. We did it right there, up against that window. He spread my arms and legs as if he was a police officer. They he gently caressed me from my neck to my inner thighs. At first I was scared out of my mind, my naked body up against that window. Anyone looking out of their window could see us. They didn't know us, and I would never see them again, is what he told me. I tried not to look down, but once I relaxed and let go, I didn't care. I was with Dashad, and he wouldn't let anything happen to me. We went from up against the window, to the couch, to the bed, and to the sink in the bathroom. I was glad that he was done with me after that, because I had no more energy to do anything. I lay on the fluffy bed and tried to get comfortable. Dashad was in the bathroom; I could hear him on the phone. He was speaking with her, and she was fussing because he hadn't been there all night. He informed her that he would be there shortly. She hung up. He came out of the bathroom and lay down with me. We fell asleep together, just how I wanted it. I would never have thought my night would end up like this.

It was late afternoon when we awoke. We ordered room service and watched movies. He told me he had to go, but wanted me to stay. I asked him how he was leaving: hadn't he gotten a ride here? He smiled and said he had driven—that was the only way he knew to get me down here. He knew I wouldn't leave him stranded. He told me he would be back for me and would take care of everything downstairs with the front desk clerk for another night. He left me $100 for room service and told me not to leave the room. He would be back.

He never came back, but I really enjoyed myself. It was a mini-vacation away from *everybody*. I didn't need or want for anything. I felt like royalty: waited on hand and foot, doing what I wanted to, watching movies, enjoying a bubble bath in the Jacuzzi, ordering the finest food, and not having to raise a finger but by putting the fork to my mouth. There was no cleanup; there were people that did all that, even the making of the bed. It was all covered. He had a way of making things special even if he wasn't there to do it himself.

I called and talked with the children. They had gone out to eat. I always leave petty cash in the house just in case of an emergency. They had gone to some type of buffet, which was great: they got to choose what they wanted, which always made them happy, and they enjoyed themselves, taking their minds off of me.

I didn't hear from him at all that night. I would imagine that he had to make things right with Stephanie. My thought was that he couldn't get out. I didn't care; I would see him soon. I was enjoying this view. I saw the sun rise and set on the Atlantic Ocean. I enjoyed peace, which I needed desperately.

I left the next afternoon as scheduled. When I walked out of that room I felt like a new me. I went to the front desk to inform them I was leaving. It was the same clerk, and I thanked her for the stay. She said she hoped to see me again soon. *Let's hope*, I thought. Three hundred dollars a night was steep, but well worth it.

On the way home, I did the math: four hundred dollars to get into the club to find me, forty to use the two cell phones, plus whatever he tipped the cashier clerk for letting him charge his phone. Sixty for perfume, six hundred for the hotel, and one-fifty for room service. Dashad had spent well over a thousand dollars on me—that was a trip to Islands. I felt like I had just gotten back from there, too. I was super-relaxed, thanks to Dashad. I did accept his apology, with a smile. He had gone through all that trouble for me. I had to forgive him. I was hoping that this would be the last time I *needed* to forgive him, but with Dashad you never knew. I left a message on his phone that I was home and for him to call me when he could.

Chapter Ten

The Things We Accept, Be the Things We Regret

The restaurant was so busy, so many parties. It was the holidays, and there were so many things to complete. There wasn't much time to go out of town or go anywhere. I stayed close to home. Dashad would come visit me and the children a couple times a week. We would have dinner and game night. Aurora was over a lot, now that she was back from down south. It was like we were young all over again.

I had lost touch with a lot of my friends; Dashad really didn't want me to have friends, but he couldn't keep me from my family. It was a blessing that Aurora had moved back. I had needed and missed her a lot. She was like my twin; she understood what I was going through. She had the same problem with James: everybody was in their business all the time. They hadn't gotten a fair shot in a relationship, so they had moved away to build their foundation. Dashad and I didn't have that luxury. My family had started to figure things out—they weren't stupid—but they kept out of it.

My mother had a long talk with me. She expressed her concerns and said that she felt bad for us. He was between fences. He loved both of us. It was hard for him to make a choice, but she told me to be ready when he made that choice—because it would be her. He had a history with her, and they had a family. "It's not to take away from what you have, but those are his children," she told me. "As a man, it is what he must do protect and provide for them." My mother always had a way of softening a blow. I loved her for that, among the many other reasons. I took in what she said and tried to mentally prepare myself for the day that Dashad and I would be over. *How do you really do that?* I wondered. In the back of my mind, I knew they were all wrong: he was here forever, just like he told me. Would I put up with this forever, being the other woman?

I was excited that today was the Alicia Keys concert at the Borgotta in Atlantic City. I called Aurora to see what she was wearing to the event. I told her to be on time, because I didn't want to have to fight for my seat. Dashad had paid a lot of money for these tickets, and Alicia Keys is one of my favorite singers. I love everything about her. It's like I could have collaborated on some of her songs. It was my life on her CDs—"If I Was Your Woman," "Diary," "Falling." I was so excited I called Dashad up to see what his plans were, to see if he could meet us after the show for dinner and to go to the casinos. His phone rang once, and then someone other than Dashad answered. It was her.

"Hello?" she said.

"Hello?" I replied, looking at the phone to see if I dialed the right number. Of course I had dialed the right number.

"Who is this?" she questioned.

"I'm sorry, I must have dialed the wrong number," I said, holding in my anger that she was answering his phone. And on top, of that I had to be nice to the bitch. I would do anything D asked, but this was killing me. He told me to just hang up, not to speak with her: it made it worse on him. This affected me.

"Who are you looking for?"

"I dialed the wrong number." I hung up.

Two minutes later, Dashad called my phone back. "Hello?" he said.

"Hello." I figured it was cool for us to talk.

"Hello?" he asked again. "Who is this?"

I couldn't believe it: he was acting like he didn't know me. I played the role, but now I was heated.

"I'm sorry sir, I told the lady that I dialed the wrong number," I said nicely. I could hear her in the background, fussing, and him telling her it was a wrong number. I hung up mad as hell. I couldn't believe he had tried to play me like that over that ugly bitch. I hated him. Whatever—I wasn't going to let it get me down, today was my day. I was going to see Alicia Keys live: fourth row, thanks to that niggah. Yep, that shit he just pulled made him one of those.

I called Aurora and told her what had happened, and she said to forget about it. She was right. I wasn't going to let them get the best of me. She was on her way over; she had several different outfits and didn't know what she should wear. Just like that, it was forgotten. When she got here, we drank wine and laughed while she tried on the many outfits she had brought for the evening. I only had two choices, because I had narrowed it down last week with the girls. I chose the black backless one-piece jumper, with my hair pulled back in a sophisticated long ponytail. It was the best low-maintenance hairstyle: I looked like Beyoncé in *Ring the Alarm*. I wore open-toed shoes so you could see my pretty, well-manicured feet. Aurora chose black slacks and a black and pink shirt, with this sharp pink hat. We stood out. Just what we needed to be noticed. We got dressed, and we were sharp. Amirah came down just before we left and told us that we both looked nice. Before we walked out the door, Aurora told me again, "Don't worry about him, we're going to have a blast. I know, easier said than done, but we're going to see Alicia Keys!" Aurora loved her like I did. She gave me a hug and thanked me for taking her. I told her I was glad that she could go and hang out with me. I knew that he would have had me sitting waiting for him, and I would have missed the show. He knew it too, which is why he suggested that I bring someone along.

As we were getting into the car, my neighbor was taking in her groceries. She shouted, "Go ahead, girl, you look good!" I thanked her, smiled, and waved. We were on the highway, listening to Alicia Keys' CD, and I was so psyched. My cell rang. It was the house, so I answered it—"Yeah?"—thinking it was one of the kids wanting something. I was wrong. It was him.

"Hello," he said, all calm and smooth.

"Hello," I said, as if nothing had happened this afternoon.

"I came here to see if I could catch you before you left. I wanted to see you. Amirah said you looked really nice."

"You should have called," I said sarcastically.

"What are you doing after the concert?"

"Don't know yet."

"What time are you coming home?"

"I don't know, why?"

"I want to talk to you."

"About what?"

"I am not going to go back and forth."

"We're almost here. I'll call you back."

I know what he was trying to do: he was trying to upset me so that I wouldn't have a good time. This was my treat, and nothing could upset me. Nothing.

We arrived. There were so many people. Everyone was dressed up, and you could tell they were just as excited as we were. We found our seats without a problem. We were just on time, because she came out on stage right after we got there. Everyone started screaming. She looked amazing, as always. She greeted everyone and started singing her ballads. Not too far into the concert, I started missing him. Certain songs that she sang would bring up feelings for him, memories of moments that we shared together. There was a couple that stood up and kissed while she sang "If I Ain't Got You." It felt so special to be a part of this, even though it made me miss him more because he should have been there holding me, kissing me.

The concert ended, and we decided to go get some dinner before we hit the tables. I called home and checked on my kids; Aurora did the same. I spoke to Amirah. I asked what Dashad had said to her. She told me he had just asked who I had left with and how I had looked—was I pretty. He had stayed there for a while with them, ordered Chinese, and left soon after Anya went to sleep. I told her I would see her in the morning and that I loved them.

Just as we were standing there deciding where to eat, I saw four of his friends. It was funny, because it was like a domino effect: one saw me, then the other, and so on. They all spoke, smiling like I knew I had no business down here looking as good as I looked without D. I smiled and waved and exited as fast as I could. I told my cousin, "Let's eat at the first restaurant we see open, then go to the marina so we can gamble there. Dashad and I always win big there. Plus the tables are cheaper than at the Borgotta."

We found a restaurant and were seated. We were looking over the menus when my cell started ringing. I knew who it was even before I looked at it. I knew that his friends had called him up and told him I was out here looking fierce. He was going crazy in his mind. I ignored his calls until we were halfway through our meals. I wanted to enjoy my evening. Dashad had made his decision this morning to ignore me, so I would return the favor and ignore him right back.

"Yes!" I shouted.

"Where are you?" he demanded.

"Where are *you*?" I questioned back.

"On my way there."

I was quiet for a second; I didn't know what to say.

"Hello?"

"Yeah."

"What are you doing?"

"We're finishing up with our meals. Why?"

"Call me when you're done, or I'll call you once I get there."

"OK." I hung up and apologized for the disruption.

My cousin thought all of this was funny. He was really tripping because he knew he had messed up and I had the right to talk to any man down here. I was looking so nice I could have had my pick. I wonder what they had said to him for him to be such in a rush to get to me.

We continued to talk, and my cousin let me in on a secret. She said everybody deals with something or other in a relationship. It's what you can handle. Once you start to lose yourself, you need to rise up out of that situation. James had cheated on her while they were down south, and he had a daughter close to her twins' age. She said she was devastated, but they had worked on it. "It is rough sometimes," she said, "but I love him and have forgiven him. Yes, he did mess up terribly, but we love each other. And it isn't the child's fault." He would have to work harder now to provide for four children her three and his one. "If you can't deal with it, then leave," she continued, "but if it's not really affecting you and you want to be with Dashad, and then be with him. Don't worry what everyone else says. He loves you, you can tell that. No man acts this way over someone that he doesn't care about. He has a situation, yes, but that is his situation, not yours. Stop letting her affect you. I am not telling you to be the other woman and let your life go by: live, love, and laugh. When that stops, it's time to go."

That was so real and interesting. I love my cousin. She always has my back, no matter what. We sat and drank some more of my favorite wine, Sangria. I had four glasses by myself. She told me that I should hang out with him tonight. She didn't mind; she would be fine driving back home. "He's in the doghouse, and he wants out. He'll do whatever he needs to do to get out." If she were me, she told me, she would enjoy that.

Just then he called my phone. I explained to him we were just finishing up. I told him that Aurora was going to head home, and asked him where he wanted to meet me. He said the rooftop. I walked my cousin to the car and thanked her again for the advice and for just being her. I repeatedly said I was sorry, but she wasn't worried about it. She didn't need any apology, I hugged her, and she got in the car and drove off.

As I walked to the elevator, I wondered what this night would bring. I phoned him on the way to the rooftop, but he had changed the plans. He wanted me to meet him in this club in the casino. He would join me there shortly.

So I did. I went in and sat down and had an apple martini. I was there about ten minutes before Dashad showed up. When I saw him, my insides got warm. I know I was supposed to be mad, but I loved him. He walked up to me, giving me some distance, and said hello, but in a weird way—as if he didn't know me. I said hello back, and he asked if anyone was sitting there. He introduced himself as Anthony. *Oh I get it*, I thought, *we're role-playing.* I told him no. He asked my name. I told him it was Anna. He sat down and started to talk about his evening. He was here from out of town, and he seemed to have lost his friends. He asked a lot of questions, and I answered them as if he didn't know the answers. After I finished my drink, he asked if he could buy me another, I agreed. Before too long, we were laughing and joking. He asked me to dance, and we got on the dance floor and had ourselves a good time. It was funny because I was so into myself that it was a while before I noticed that I was dancing alone. He was just standing there watching me. I smiled. He excused himself to the bathroom. I sat back down and ordered a bottle of water. I needed it. I had been drinking wine all day with Aurora, and now I had just had two apple martinis. I needed to slow down. He came back over to the table as the real Dashad. He was so funny. He was apologizing for being late: the concert traffic was really heavy. He commented on how nice I looked. He went on about Amirah telling him I looked nice, but not saying I looked that nice. I sucked it right up. You can never get too many compliments. He asked me how many men had tried to talk to me while I was sitting there, and I told him just one guy: "He had potential, too, but I am in love with someone else, so I told him to get lost." I just looked at him and smiled. He smiled back. He said it was time to go. When we got on the elevator, he told me again how pretty I looked this evening and asked me questions about the concert. I leaned over and kissed him on the mouth. We kissed all the way until we reached the rooftop, where his car was. I was hot and wanted him. He said he had a surprise for me when we got to the car. It was a dozen red roses. I thanked him but told him that he was going to have to do better than that. He assured me that he would. It was still early.

We decided we would go back downstairs and gamble a little, and both of us were winning. I went to the bathroom to freshen up and noticed I had two missed calls and a message. It was Cynthia the nanny: Amir was running a high fever. I told Dashad I would have to take a rain check, and we hurried home.

We went to the emergency room, where they told us he had the flu. They treated him with some antibiotics and sent him home with us. I told D he could go, but he wanted to stay. Amir was his little man, and he wanted to make sure he was OK.

Dashad went home early that morning. He told me he would be back later on. Two days before Christmas, he called and told me that he had deposited a thousand dollars into my account. He wanted me to get the children and myself something nice. He wouldn't be here for the holiday, but he would definitely be here for New Year's. We had a very nice Christmas; my family came over, and it was just so special. I was so busy with all the visitors that I only thought of Dashad a couple of times. I explained to the children that he was out of town. I don't think they really cared; they were just happy with all the gifts they received—which was a lot. I got myself a tennis bracelet from Dashad. Everyone oohed and aahed. It was nice, if I do say so myself. He called that night after everyone had left and the children had gone to sleep. I gave him all the details and told him what gifts he had gotten the children. I was a little upset with him, but the children were happy, so it was all right as usual. He informed me he would make it up to me. We would get together soon. We played phone tag for the next couple days, never making any real plans for New Year's.

"Five! Four! Three! Two! Happy New Year!" we shouted to each other. Every time the phone rang, I was hoping it was D. After some time, the phone stopped ringing with New Year's salutations. We sat on the couch watching the events on television. One by one, the children fell asleep. I just sat there waiting for my call. I didn't get it. Why did he feel it was OK to disappoint me? I went to sleep.

The next day he showed up acting like he hadn't disappointed me, like everything was normal. He spoke with the kids about how their holiday had been and how he wished he could have been there with them.

Soon he came into the living room, where I was, kissed me on my forehead, and asked me how I was doing. Did I save him any pie? I didn't answer. He asked me to not be like that, he couldn't help it. Stephanie had had a New Year's party, and he hadn't found out about it until the last minute. Her family and friends were coming, so he had to be there. He let me know again that he would make it up to us. I was giving him the update on how our holiday had gone when I noticed a red mark on his neck.

"What's that?" I asked, looking at it like it was cancer or something.

"What?"

I walked him over to the mirror in the hallway. He looked in the mirror and looked back at me. He had the nerve to smile.

"*Oh, that's funny?*" I said.

"Not in the way you think; she did this on purpose."

"Oh you think?" I stormed upstairs.

He followed me. "Baby, wait!" I slammed the door right in his face: one more step, and it would have hit him. At this point, I didn't care.

He swung open the door. "What's your problem?"

"*You're* my problem. I am so tired of this shit!" I shouted.

"Why are you so worried about—?"

I cut him off. I couldn't take it anymore. I was beside myself. "You come in here with a passion mark from another woman, and you ask why I'm *worried*? Fuck her, and fuck you!" I continued to shout.

Smack, right across my mouth. "Who do you think you're talking to?" he questioned.

I looked at him right in his face and said, "That isn't going to shut me up! Get out, get out right now! I'm done with all of this shit! I deserve someone who cares and gives a shit about my feelings! Get out!"

He stood there, looking at me like I was speaking in a language he wasn't sure of. He tried to explain, but I continued to ignore him. I just wanted him to leave so I could cry my eyes out. I didn't want him to see me cry about him—or that bitch.

"Get out, get out! Just go!" I couldn't hold it in; it just burst out. It was like I had opened up a faucet. I had to let it out. I felt so betrayed: for five years I had given him everything, all of me. He could have stayed home; he could have called to check on Amir. He wanted me to see that mess on his neck. He didn't care. He never had. I was his trophy—you know the pretty one that they parade around on their arm. He didn't love me. I was more like his property, something he had, something he could control. Something that made him feel like a man. I was done, really done, this time. I was glad my mother had had that talk with me; she had prepared me for this.

"Dashad, it's over. Please leave. Say good-bye to the children and go."

I said it in the calmest voice ever. He just continued to look at me.

"I'm not going anywhere. This is my house."

"No, sweetie, this is my house. And I am asking you to leave, nicely. I'm over this love triangle. She can have your ass." I started to the bedroom door.

"Baby, wait!" I turned to look at him, and then turned back around and walked out of my bedroom.

Amirah was standing at the end of the hall. She smiled at me and went into her bedroom. That was what made me even more proud that I had made the decision. She had known all along what was going on. Don't be fooled by children: they know everything and hear everything. I guess she had trusted me enough to know that they would always be OK. I had their best interest in mind. I am glad I didn't lose respect from her—that would have killed me.

He followed me to the kitchen, trying to talk to me. I didn't want to hear it. I acted like he wasn't even there. He sat himself down at the table, looking like an ass, and just followed me with his eyes while I prepared dinner.

I was thinking to myself, *I am not losing anything. I am stronger than what I think. I can do this. I deserve my own man: one who wouldn't hurt me, who wouldn't cheat on me, and who wouldn't have any SITUATIONS. One who wouldn't hit me for ANY reason.* I didn't need him. Before I met him, I was paying my own bills, being the independent woman that I am. Yes, I deserved so much more. I had put up with Dashad for many years now, because I loved him. I needed to start loving myself.

After sitting there for about twenty minutes, he walked over to me and tried to kiss me. I leaned my head out of the way of his lips. He tried again, then kissed me on my forehead and told me he was leaving. He said he would be back. He would call me later on, once I "cooled down." He walked out the door. I was happy to see him go. The sooner I got on with my life, the better.

I phoned my mom and told her that I was taking a vacation with the children, to go see Mo. We would only be gone for a week. I needed for her to look over things while we were gone. I needed some time away to get my head back straight. I told her I had left Dashad, and left him for good. She said she was sorry to hear that, but she trusted that I knew what I was doing. She would be here if I needed her.

I then called Mo. She was happy that I had left him and that we were coming to spend some time with her. She missed us. I booked the flight for me and the children to leave that weekend. It was the best money I could have spent: one week in LA with my girl and the kids. What could be better?

I needed to get away from Dashad. I knew he would be back bothering me. I was done with him and had to give him clear signs that I meant it.

He did call me that night. I ignored it. I put signs on my bedroom wall and bathroom mirror that read, *Love yourself, pray for strength, and always know you deserve the best.*

We arrived in Los Angeles. It was so nice. The scenery was like on television: tall palm trees, wide roads. Nothing like the East coast, and just what I needed to refresh my mind. No memories, nothing linking me to him. No phones to receive calls. My mother knew Mo's number. If it was an emergency she would call her.

We enjoyed ourselves everyday of our miniature vacation. We went shopping, and visited the beach. It was so tranquil. While the children were in the water, I decided to write my last poem to Dashad, called "Baby Wait." I was trying not to think of him, but these were my last and final words.

Our vacation had ended. I was glad that I had come out to LA. I had really needed to get away, and the children had enjoyed themselves. I had cleared my mind and was ready to get back to my life. I missed the hustle and bustle just a little.

We arrived at Philadelphia International Airport to see my mother and both my brothers waiting for us to come through the gate. The children ran to see them. I was happy. I was home, and my family was right there. That's all you need when you have troubles: a little time away and your family's support.

My mother stayed the night and had a million questions. I told her that I planned to go back to LA—just me and her.

She asked me how I felt: was I ready to face him? He had called my mother and talked with her while I was gone. She said he was broken up about the whole thing. She said she had just listened and told him just give me a minute to myself; maybe things would work out for the best. I told her there would be no getting back together. I knew he wasn't leaving Stephanie because of the kids, and I knew now that he did love her. I wanted out of that triangle. I deserved so much more. I wouldn't want him to leave his children anyway. It was better for them to try to work it out. I was proud of myself. I had made a great choice. I didn't know what the future held for me, but I knew what I *didn't* want. If I was strong enough to put up with all the stuff that I went through over the years, I would be strong enough to step out on what I knew I deserved. I deserved a loving man, one who supported me and wanted me to succeed, who was secure letting me be me, who did not want to control me.

That week, I talked to Leah. Surprisingly, she didn't come at me with the negativity, talking mess about him. She was the friend I needed. She let me know she would be there if I needed her. I was actually fine. The time away really had helped. She told me that Bryan had told her that Dashad had been sick since I left him. Not like germ sick, but sick. He was drinking a lot, not his upbeat self. I felt a little sorry for him, but this time around it had to be about me and my happiness. I had put him in front of me so long that I thought that was where I was supposed to be: in the back. What star shines in the darkness, what flower grows in the dark? None that I had ever heard of.

He called me that weekend, and I answered.

"Yes?" I said in a peaceful voice.

"How are you and the kids?"

"We're all fine."

"How was your trip?"

I was just about to ask how he had found out, but it didn't even matter to me anymore.

"We had a great time. I needed to get away and clear my mind."

"I miss . . ." I interrupted him.

"Dashad, it's over. I'm sorry, but I want more, and you can't—and won't—give it to me."

"I want to make it up to you. I admit I played a lot of games, but I had time to think. I know what I want now."

"With you, this *is* a game, and you don't want to lose right now. But really, you're not. You can make it work with her. You have a family, common goals that you need to work on for your girls. It will always be like this with us. I can't and won't trust you anymore. I have no more to give to you." I started to cry. "I love you—don't get me wrong—but it's not enough. I love myself more. I gave you five years of me to make things right, and you didn't. I was wrong to stay in the beginning, when I found out about her, but you wowed me. I thought I could never find another you. I'm doing this for me. I want you to understand that. I will always love you, but it's over."

"I want to come see you. It's not over."

"Dashad, please. If you cared anything about me, you would want the best for me. And right now, you are not it. I deserve so much more. I have to go."

"Baby, wait!"

Just then I thought of the poem.

"I do have something for you. You can come here to get it, but if you start your shit, I'll call the police."

"I'm on my way." Then he hung up.

He heard nothing that I had said: he really thought he was going to talk me out of what I wanted, and into what he wanted. He had been doing it for years now, so why would he think he couldn't change my mind? That was my fault. I decided not to let him in. He would get violent with me, like he had in past. I left the poem taped to the door, with a note.

The note read, "I am sorry, but I don't want this anymore. Take care and be well. Love, Me."

I heard him pull up. I went to my bedroom window to see him. He got out of the car and walked up the walkway. As he got closer, he saw the note and the poem taped to the storm door. He pulled both down and read the note first. He crumpled the note and threw it in my flowers. He looked up at the window to see if I was looking out at him. He couldn't see me, but he still knew me. He began to read.

Baby Wait

You drowned me in fear as I lay my head into a pillow soaked with tears and as I started to realize my mistakes you said . . . Baby Wait!

You made me think blue was green and my reality was a dream, and as I fixed my mouth to scream you said . . .

Baby Wait!

You kissed my happiness to hell with the attitude of oh well and as I became overwhelmed you said . . .
Baby Wait!

I separated the real from the fake not knowing you were in the wrong category, and before I could tell another sad story you said . . .
Baby Wait!

You messed up, I looked past and knowing what you had you constantly cheated with trash, and when I said I had enough you weren't feeling too tough so you said . . .
Baby Wait . . .

You made me feel like I just couldn't cut it, and anything you wanted if you liked it I loved it, and when I tried to turn away you said . . .
Baby Wait . . .

I accepted your flaws with my heart paying the cost while you were out playing boss, my mind was lost, and when I said I need you now you were nowhere to be found and as I turned around you said . . .
Baby Wait . . .

Mind, body, and soul beaten while you in strip clubs freaking with hoes and the shit they do every night only God knows but as you proposed to tell me you were innocent I took a minute to pack my things and you said . . .
Baby Wait!

No phone calls, no affection and when you not home who you sexing? I'm constantly waiting on you all the time and as I got tired of losing my mind you said . . .
Baby Wait!

What about my feelings?

What about my heart?
What about my mind? Do you even care that you're out of line? Or better yet, what about me, I constantly ask, and you just laugh so I kissed your lips good-bye and you said . . .
Baby Wait!

Now it's too late.

    I guess he read it twice, because he stood there for a minute, looking at the paper. He shocked me, because he looked right up at the window where I was and asked, "It's too late?" he paused for a second, then he turned and walked down the walkway. I felt like someone had died. This was it, the end. I never thought I would see this day. No more me and Dashad. He got in the car and drove off. I lay on the bed and cried. I would miss him, but I had to let him go. I would have died—emotionally, mentally, or maybe even physically, with his temper.

Chapter Eleven

Let Me Reintroduce Myself

I got up the next morning feeling beat. I looked in the mirror. My eyes were swollen from crying all night. I read my little note on the mirror again: *Love yourself, pray for strength to get you through, and always know you deserve the best*. I washed my face, brushed my teeth, and got in the shower. The water felt different that day. I let it all go. I was a free woman: free from doubt, heartache, and lies, able to do what I wanted. It felt good. There was no turning back now. I knew what direction I was going in, and from here on out, I was going to stay focused.

When I left the house that day, it was cold out, but it was beautiful. The sun was shining so brightly it was like God was smiling on me. Everything seemed new and fresh. I did things again my way, making myself happy. When you are happy, your children and loved ones are happy, too.

I got to work feeling like a new woman. My mom said she could even see the difference. I went into my office and saw a big bouquet of lilies on my desk. They were truly beautiful, white and pink. Some of the them were open, and it made the office smell lovely. My mom walked in behind me. "They are nice," She said.

"Yes, they are." *That was sweet of him*, I thought. *I think I'll put them out front for the customers to enjoy*. I put them out front, walked back to my office, and carried on with my day. I felt like a stranger in my own establishment, but it didn't matter. I was back. I would not lose my way again.

I knew he would be calling me, so I decided to change my number. I called my cellular carrier and asked that my number be changed to something similar to the number I had, and right away. It took a while, but she gave me a number that was only two numbers off from my old one. I took it gladly. I informed my mother of the change, and sent a text out to everyone in my phone except his family. I couldn't trust it. I needed to heal without the drama. The worst part was over, and the healing process needed to begin.

Sad to say but this was a familiar place to me. I just wanted to stay busy all the time so I wouldn't think of him much. It hurt like hell. There were days I wanted to just die. I kept it moving. I decided to remodel the house and the restaurant. Those two projects would keep me occupied for months. It would definitely keep me busy, and keep my mind off of what I was going through.

Once I was over most of the hurt, I sat down and had a long talk with Amirah and Amir. I let them in on things that were way beyond their maturity level. I had to let them know that Dashad was no longer part of our lives. He was not allowed in the house, and if they saw him, they were to let me know at once. This was the rule no matter *where* they saw him: at school, at the restaurant, in the mall—anywhere. It was understood how I felt and what was expected of them. This was for their protection as well as mine.

I worked out more than before. I went to the gym three times a week and did Pilates at home on the weekend with Aurora.

Every day, I had to build myself back up, build my self-worth. I had to stay focused this time. I had no more time to lose. He had disrespected me because I had disrespected myself. I should have had the faith in myself to know better. No matter how much he had to offer, I should not have allowed any man to have me in that—*Jerry Springer episode*. I was too good for that. No woman deserved to be treated that way. If we knew our worth, I realized, others would recognize it and respect it.

The weather was changing. It was spring, just what I needed: the beautiful array of flowers to keep me in good spirits. Aurora and I decided to go out shopping for spring clothes and jackets with the children. We chose to go shopping on South Street. I could get everything for everybody in one shot. It was an excellent idea. The day was lovely, until Nya noticed Dashad across the street. Before we could get her attention, she shouted his name. He was shopping with *his* family. He turned around and looked. He saw us. *She* didn't notice or hear Anya; she was already on her way into a store. I grabbed Nya and told her that she had seen someone who looked like Dashad, not him.

We continued to walk down the crowded street. I never looked back. I suggested ice cream for the kids. We ordered the ice cream, sat down, and enjoyed our frozen treats. Not long after, I saw Dashad on the other side of the street—*without* his family and looking for mine. He was still up to no good. He could have just let it go, knowing that we were doing well. He had gotten to see all of us, OK. No, not him. He wanted to erase all the mending to unravel it again. But I wasn't going to let him. I told Aurora to stay with the children: I was going to put the bags in the truck. She knew what was going on. She knew I had to do this. He was walking in the same direction as my truck. If I knew Dashad like I thought, he was already looking for my truck.

Once I walked around the corner, guess who was at my truck? Yup. I just looked at him. I thought, *this is the same man that I once loved.* I was so over him. Inside, I was jumping up and down, I was so pleased with myself. My heart wanted him no more. I knew I deserved better than his cheating ass. He had a nerve to smile when he saw me. I stood there with the stone face.

"Isis."

"Dashad."

"You look good." *What?* I thought. *I'm supposed to be all messed up because you hurt me to my core. Oh no, brother I am back and over you. I am that independent, determined, sexy, seeing-clearer-than-I-have-been-in-years mother of three beautiful children that you met five years ago. But with more self worth than you can imagine.*

"I came to tell you not to say anything to the children. It took a lot to undo the hurt we inflicted on them. I am done with you. I wish you no harm. But, Dashad, you are a chapter in my book that has ended. I don't want my children to hurt any more than what they already have. You're wrong for wanting to open up those wounds with them and me. You're selfish. I didn't come here to name-call, but it is what it is. You take care of yourself." I shut the back door to my truck and walked off. He was just standing there, stuck. I wanted to add more, but that would have meant I still cared and was not over him. And I *was* over him. I had gotten it off my chest—not that I had to. If I never saw him again, I would have been blessed still.

I turned the corner, very proud of myself. I had made a very good decision for me and my family. As I went into the ice cream parlor, they were just finishing up. It was perfect timing. It was time to get out of there. As we were about to exit the store, Nya shouted, "There goes the man that looks like Dashad." We all looked at each other and laughed. That day, I stood with my head held very high. I was very proud of myself and the decisions I had made. I drove off with the thought, *The Divas That We Are!*